HOW TO FIGHT ISLAMIST TERROR FROM THE MISSIONARY POSITION

HOW TO FIGHT ISLAMIST TERROR FROM THE MISSIONARY POSITION

A NOVEL

TABISH KHAIR

Interlink Books

An imprint of Interlink Publishing Group, Inc.
Northampton, Massachusetts

First American edition published in 2014 by

INTERLINK BOOKS
An imprint of Interlink Publishing Group, Inc.
46 Crosby Street, Northampton, Massachusetts 01060
www.interlinkbooks.com

ISBN 978-1-56656-946-0 (hb)   ISBN 978-1-56656-970-5 (pb)

Library of Congress Cataloging-in-Publication Data
Khair, Tabish.
How to Fight Islamist Terror from the Missionary Position / by Tabish Khair. -- First edition.
    pages cm
ISBN 978-1-56656-970-5
1. Single men--Fiction. 2. Life change events--Fiction. 3. Denmark--Fiction. 4. Satire. I. Title.
PR9499.3.K427H69 2013
823'.92--dc23
                        2013023658

Printed and bound in the United States of America
10 9 8 7 6 5 4 3 2 1

To request a copy of our 48-page full-color catalog, please call 1-800-238-LINK, visit our website at www.interlinkbooks.com, or write to:
Interlink Publishing, 46 Crosby Street, Northampton, MA 01060
info@interlinkbooks.com

With thanks to Sam Selvon and Dany Laferrière

CONTENTS

PROLEGOMENON TO A PLOT

Always begin in medias res, said the only girl I ever fucked who had an MFA in writing (from an American university). At the moment she gave me that bit of advice about writing, we were almost in the middle of something else and consequently the rest of her advice was cut short or has since slipped my memory.

Having set myself the task of providing a full account of the events that have exercised considerable media attention in Denmark in recent months and that involved me, though not mentioned by name, I now wish that I had paid more attention to her words and less attention to her. This, however, was difficult.

But whatever she or her MFA professors might have said, I am certain that this account starts one winter morning on Kastelsvej, which is a desolate suburban street off the main road leading from Århus to Randers, where I sat behind the steering wheel of a parked Hyundai i10, engine running for warmth, and tried desperately to jerk off into a plastic container with a label bearing the name and social security number of my wife. This was a little over two years ago.

I had ten minutes to fill the container to the best of my capacity and drive it to the fertility clinic, which was just around the corner and would be opening at seven, in exactly ten minutes. Then I had an hour to drive to a high school in Randers, a forty-five-minute drive in light traffic, where I was supposed to deliver a guest lecture at eight. Hence the desperation.

The fact that these plastic containers are made by someone with a rather optimistic idea of the productive capacity of man did not help. The fact that I had been following this routine for more than six months did not help. And the fact that a patrol car was slowly cruising the main road in the morning haze did not help at all.

I prayed to the God I did not believe in that the patrol car would cruise on and not turn into a desolate side street with a Hyundai i10 parked in it, its engine running. Even as I duly submitted my prayer in triplicate, I knew it stood no chance. It was bound to be rejected. No self-respecting patrol car could ignore such a target of investigation so early in the morning. Doing my best with one hand to keep to my schedule, I observed the car in my rearview mirror. It slowed down. Then its left indicator winked hazily and its headlights cut through the fog into my street.

My heart sank. If this particular cop found the sight of a law-abiding Japanese or Far Asian car suspicious, parked no matter where and how, what would he think when he discovered that the driver of the car was a more or less Muslim-skinned man? The excitement of the situation must have helped, for at that very moment my beleaguered appendage sent an SOS of sensation back to me, a silent version of the whistle that old-fashioned trains let off in old-fashioned films before they start pulling out of old-fashioned stations. Did I have the time to let this train pull out and cap the evidence before the patrol car pulled up? And if I did, would I be able to get my clarifications in place quickly enough to make it to the clinic and then to my lecture, for which I was going to be paid money that my gaily mortgaging bank could use in these times of financial crisis?

I had to make a quick decision. And suddenly, after months of indecision, I knew what I had to do. I looked at the name on that ambitious plastic container. I said, in my heart or perhaps even audibly, I am sorry. I might even have said: no more. I zipped up. Then I slowly pressed the clutch, changed the gear, waved nonchalantly at the cops in the patrol car, and drove back home.

If I had not said sorry at that moment and definitely if I had not said "no more" later on, I would not have gotten divorced. And if I had not gotten divorced, I would not have started sharing a flat with Karim and Ravi. And if I had not started sharing a flat with Karim and Ravi, the account that I am going to give you—which is a more complex version of what you might have read in the papers—would not have been necessary.

So in medias res or coitus interruptus or whatever else in Latin Ravi might suggest, this is where it all started.

I had known Ravi for three years, ever since I moved to Århus with my English wife. This was when, having completed a PhD at Surrey, I was offered my first full-time position, with the carrot of tenure tied to its stick of pedagogic overwork. Following my divorce, with my wife heading back to Guildford in Surrey, Ravi and I decided to save money and rent a flat together. Ravi had just been politely kicked out of his fifth flat in fewer years; this time, he proclaimed, for putting too much (fried) garlic into his food.

He claimed that he had been asked to leave, politely, for playing (mostly Maghrebi) music too loud, frying his food instead of boiling it, walking about in his undergarments, using too much (fried) spice in his cooking, and not cleaning his windows—in that order—in the past. Of course, those were never the reasons given, Ravi confessed under intensive cross-examination by my (now ex-) wife; the reasons given were always polite ones. Dammit, yaar, he said to me later, this is not a bloody Third World state; it is a civilized country. You think anyone would give you real reasons in a civilized place? On one occasion, he conceded, it might also have had to do with him encouraging his landlady's barkative poodle down the stairs at a rather precipitous pace. But, in general, Ravi maintained, his food, music and clothing had a role to play in his gypsy status in Århus. Not that my ex-wife had believed his stories. "Can you imagine anyone throwing Ravi out, in any country?" she had asked me, alluding to the ease of assurance that Ravi exuded. "He must set out to provoke these poor people."

It was while we were doing the rounds looking for places to rent—our university background prevented us from going for one of those "udlænding ghettoes" where Ravi's cooking would have been tolerated—that we met Karim. At forty-five, Karim was more than a decade older than us. He had a full flowing beard, speckled with grey. Like Ravi, he was an Indian; like me, he was a Muslim. Unlike me, he believed in God and his prophets, especially the very last one; unlike Ravi, he did not get worked up about what the West had been doing to all the rest, as Ravi liked to put it. But let me not jump the gun. There is probably a MFA rule against it that, I am sure, I would know if I had paid more attention to my MFA girlfriend of yore. Let me commence with our meeting Karim.

This was about a year after my fatal encounter with the cruising patrol car: my separation and divorce did not take place instantly, it need hardly be said. But a year later, divorce filed for, mortgaged flat sold at a slight loss, mortgaged car sold at a significant loss, (almost ex-) wife departed to Ye Olde England, Ravi and I decamped from an overpriced flat-to-rent with a caring property agent showering brochures on us with the avidity of relieved family members strewing rice on the bride. We were late. Our next meeting, with another property agent, was on the other side of the town.

We jumped into the first taxi we came across. Karim was the taxi driver. His beard fooled Ravi into thinking that Karim was from

Pakistan, like me, or Afghanistan, like the Italians in our favorite Italian pizzeria, Milano, on Borgmester Erik Skous Allé. Ravi believes in maintaining good neighborly relations: he might rudely ignore fellow Indians, but he always pulls out his most chaste Urdu, knots it like an old school tie for identification and prestige, and launches into intricate conversations with Pakistanis. Within minutes these conversations dive into private matters with a comfortable inquisitiveness that would do credit to any of my aunts. We were only halfway through town before Karim and Ravi were exchanging the nicknames of their third cousins and remarking on the fact that while Hindu and Muslim names in the subcontinent mostly differ, the nicknames usually tally. Or Ravi was remarking on it; Karim was nodding politely.

When we exited the overpriced, under-spaced flat we had rushed to investigate, dodging the brochures showered on us by another property agent, and came out on the street, Karim's taxi was still parked by the curb. Karim was standing there, rolling a cigarette. Ravi went over for a farewell chat and a final exchange of nicknames of distant cousins. I stayed where I was. A cold wind was blowing, reducing audibility. I could only catch a word or two of their conversation. I could see it was getting chummier and chummier. Or Ravi was, as Karim was a friendly but reserved man. Very soon Ravi was clapping Karim on his shoulder. Then the two of them did a kind of Eid Mubarak hug.

Ravi came back to me with a broad smile on his handsome Bollywood-star face. I have never met anyone with a broader smile than Ravi's, when he decides to let it rip. He did that day. Guess what, bastard, he said to me. Bastard was a term of affection between us, as it usually is in the subcontinent between men who share a Catholic missionary-school education. Guess what, bastard, Ravi said, I have found us a fucking flat.

As I blinked up to him in wonderment—I am not short, but Ravi is a bit over six—he explained: Karim Bhai there, he has rooms to rent in his flat, and I think we should take them.

Ravi's enthusiasm faltered when we entered Karim Bhai's flat. Yes, it was that flat: the flat that was mentioned—in lieu of our legally protected names—in all the tabloids when it happened. As you probably know from the newspapers, the flat was well situated, on the third floor of a building on a quiet street. It had a small balcony that looked out over the street, onto a park. You have probably seen photos of the flat and the building from so many angles. No, location or convenience was not the problem. The problem was that it was a two-bedroom flat. Two bedrooms, a larger living room, with a small lobby between them, a kitchen with space for a table with four chairs, and a cramped bathroom and toilet.

In his windswept conversation with Karim, Ravi had got the impression that there were two rooms to rent. Now, he looked down at Karim—the shortest of the three of us—and said, with just a touch of irritation, "Karim Bhai, we are in the humanities, I know, but we are not completely gay."

Karim looked like he had been slapped. He was not a man who joked about too many things.

"Allah forbid," he said, slapping himself lightly on both cheeks, the first time I had seen this traditional gesture of repentance performed anywhere except in a historical Bombay flick, "Such an indecent thought would never cross my mind, Ravi Bhai."

Karim peered at us from wide staring eyes. He had baby eyes: round and a bit dilated, as if in surprise, with slightly darkened edges. In all the months we shared his flat with him, I could never determine if the darkened edges were natural or due to the application of kohl that, though uncommon now, was once widely used by men in north India. I knew Ravi had gone too far. Karim was not from the kind of circles where sexuality was a matter of choice—or irreverence. I hastened to explain to Karim that Ravi's joke was his way of mentioning that we wanted to rent separate rooms.

"Separate rooms. Of course, yes, of course. See," said Karim, with relief writ large on his face, "see, there are two bedrooms." He gestured towards the doors of the bedrooms on the other side of the small lobby.

"But you, Karim Bhai? Don't you live here too?"

"Yes, yes, I do," said Karim Bhai. "I live in the third room." He gestured at the living room.

We could now see that clothes hung in the living room, ready on hangers. There was no bed in it. But there was a large sagging resin-covered sofa on which were piled sheets and pillows. Evidently, unlike us, Karim Bhai came from those sections of the working class that are accustomed to sleeping regularly on sofas.

And accustomed he was, as we were later to find out. He had been sleeping on the sofa for years now, ever since he rented out the bedrooms for the first time. This was soon after he had bought the flat, from a bankruptcy sale, and restored it with his own hands. That he rented out the rooms for money was something he did not hide from us. That he needed the money was also something he was not ashamed to confess. But the purpose for which he needed the money remained, alas, a secret to us until the last moments of the crisis that broke over our heads and so exercised the Danish media and politicians for a few weeks.

At that moment, I recall, Ravi asked him about the previous incumbents.

"Oh, they just left a week ago," said Karim Bhai evasively.

"Some of their things are still here; they will collect them some day."

Given Ravi's aunty-like probing, it was soon revealed, over cups of Darjeeling tea that Karim Bhai brewed for us in the kitchen, that the previous renters had been a family of refugees from ex-Yugoslavia: the parents were old Tito-supporters and die-hard atheists, despite being Muslims; the daughter, at eighteen, had discovered Islam through Karim Bhai and the local mosque. When she wanted to marry a young Muslim man from Somalia, whom she had met at the same mosque, the parents threw a tantrum. More, hinted Karim Bhai disapprovingly, because of the man's intense faith than because of his color. The girl married her lover and moved in with him. The parents moved out soon afterwards. The things that lay about in Karim's flat were mostly the girl's. She had promised to collect them.

This story gave Ravi cause for pause. He looked at me thoughtfully, sipping tea from the flowery china cup that had probably been bought in Bazar Vest or carted back from India, for no Danish supermarket could have stocked such a gaudy non-European brand. I knew what he was thinking. But I was not going to help him out. This was his idea. Let the bastard sweat it out.

Then Ravi made up his mind and decided to grab the bull by the horns.

"You see, Karim Bhai," he began hesitantly, "we like your place, and the rent you have quoted suits us. But you see, you are like an older brother, and we would not like to cause you pain. We are, how shall I put it, single men, and you know that single men sometimes like to be visited by women and open a bottle of wine for inspiration. Our own Ghalib wrote, and that was probably when he was no longer so young, jo haathon mein jumbish nahin..."

Karim Bhai ignored the bit about women and Ghalib. He never liked to say anything about women, if he could help it, as we discovered later. But he answered Ravi's question.

He replied: "What you do in your rooms is between you and Allah. But not a drop in my room, if you call me your brother. In my room, I pray."

That is how we came to rent Karim Bhai's flat.

POSTURES OF PRAYER

Karim Bhai folded up his prayer mat and put it in the corner where it always stood. Ravi observed with interest. Within a week of having moved into Karim's flat, Ravi had convinced him of his desire to learn the Muslim prayer. It was a desire he had revealed to me months ago, only to be rebuffed by my laughter and the news that I had not said the prayer for almost two decades. Even in the days when I accompanied my father to Eid prayers, twice a year, I did my genuflections by adhering to the precedence set by those around me. When the person to the left bowed, so did I. When the person to the right stood up, so did I. For years I admired the people praying around me for their ability to remember the intricate and shifting maneuvers of the Islamic prayer, in its many combinations and forms. Then, at the age of sixteen or seventeen, following a bet with an older cousin, I discovered that my admiration was at least a bit misplaced. The cousin had suggested that most people did the Eid prayers by copying their neighbors. Try it out, he said; do the wrong thing just a second before, and you will see. I did. I saw. Half the row to my left and at least three people to my right copied my deliberate mistake before they corrected themselves.

So, apart from the incongruity of tall, elegant, clean-shaven, all-rules-barred Ravi, as twice-born a Hindu as any Brahmin, doing his best to be a meticulous impure Muslim—he had confessed that the only Muslims he really knew as a child were (out-house) servants of the family—I was simply unable to provide him with the necessary guidance. Karim Bhai was not so religiously challenged. He performed the pre-prayer wazu as the sort of art that it was meant to be in deserts with little water; he knew his surahs inside out; he did not need to sneak a glance to the left or the right before going into sijda or standing up. That he agreed to supervise Ravi surprised me, but then I understood: as a religious Muslim, he could not refuse such a request. It was enjoined on all Muslims to preach the final and unalloyed word of God. To convert a non-Muslim to Islam is to be shown the secret side door to paradise. How could Karim Bhai have refused Ravi?

Teaching time, he now announced to Ravi.

Clear out, shameless degenerate, Ravi said to me. He did not want me around because he claimed that my smirk disturbed his concentration. I continued reading the Proust (in translation) that I was re-reading, as an antidote to teaching literature in the English Department of Århus University.

Karim Bhai was a good trainer. He put Ravi through his paces. He was calm, determined and precise. As the Muslim prayers come with different combinations of verses and postures, I knew that Ravi had a long education ahead of him. And a painful one, for some of the postures are remarkably hard to maintain for more than a few seconds.

Later that evening, on our way to Under Masken, almost the only bar in town that allowed one to smoke in peace, Ravi groaned. "Now I understand why you fucking mullahs came over and colonized us. It was not the gunpowder and the cannons. It was the namaaz. While we were sitting around on our backsides, jingling bells at our gods, you were working out five times a day. The namaaz is the gym of Islam; that's why they hate it so much in the West. It is too much competition for their fucking health businesses."

Ravi was never as reverent about my religion when he was with me as he was with Karim Bhai.

It was a Thursday evening, and Under Masken was already crowded when we got there. We still had half an hour to kill before our double dates arrived. We managed to get a corner table under the usual assortment of masks and trinkets. A huge aquarium lined the wall behind us.

Ravi lit a cigarette. I had smoked occasionally, at parties or on nights out, but Ravi had started smoking just a couple of years back, when smoking was banned in public places in Denmark. He claimed the ban was proof of the sexist and anti–working-class turn of Denmark in recent years, for it was mostly women and working-class men who still smoked. He decided to oppose it by smoking at least one cigarette per day and so far he had steadfastly adhered to his sole, silent, smoking protest against the ruling powers of Denmark.

He offered me a cigarette from his packet of Marlboro. I declined. A rare smoker, I did not feel that the cigarette fog in the pub required any further contribution from me.

The women who entered, within a minute of each other, did not look very different from their photos on the dating site. That was a relief. They also appeared to be able to identify us easily, though of course any two South Asians in any bar in Århus could not be too difficult to locate. Introductions over, drinks fetched (by Ravi, the generous), our conversation hesitated and hiccupped like an antique car; then it rolled down the kind of incline that I had become familiar with over the past few months of internet dating in Denmark.

The initial weeks had been a surprise, though I'd been forewarned by Ravi, who had been religiously dating on the internet, and elsewhere, since his arrival in Denmark. Between us, he liked to point out, we had experience of dating in five countries: India, Pakistan (though Ravi had reservations about the existence of real dating in that country), England, the USA, and Switzerland. Switzerland and the USA, where he had spent various periods as student or journalist, were Ravi's contribution to the list, as was India. But Denmark, Ravi claimed, was different. It was perhaps the only country left in the Western Hemisphere where 80 percent of all women were afraid of dating a colored man and all but one percent of the rest would only date colored men if they had a chance. A bit like England in the 1950s; this progressive country is a few decades behind the rest in some areas, Ravi insisted.

At first inclined to dismiss this as predictable rhetoric from Ravi, over the past few months I'd had to concede that it did contain a kernel of truth. Now, in the music-filled smoky atmosphere of Under Masken, my conversation with my date—a tall, floridly beautiful platinum blonde, who made a striking contrast to Ravi's smaller, thinner date, a woman with a hard mouth and spiky brown hair—proceeded down familiar avenues. Ravi's date, after establishing her credentials with Ravi by criticizing the Danish People's Party and its anti-immigrant politics, had proceeded, a bit surprisingly, to launch into a detailed analysis of last night's handball semi-final between Denmark and Spain, which Denmark had won after trailing in the first quarter. I knew Ravi must be squirming in the depths of his casually clad soul, as he had no interest whatsoever in any ball game: Ravi was of the opinion that the West's fascination with ball games, sadly being communicated to the rest, was susceptible to Freudian analysis, and not necessarily from the angle of the Oedipus complex. When my platinum blonde, after mentioning her love of

Tolkien, which was perhaps evoked by the fact, glaringly mentioned in my dating profile, that I "loved, read and taught (but did not write) literature," proceeded to tell me how she never dated Danish men, who were always so incredibly boring, I knocked Ravi's knee three times with my knee. This was one of our established signals. There was a pause. Then he tapped back three times. He had agreed.

Two minutes later, I excused myself, went to the dingy little poster-ridden toilet on the other side of the bar and called Ravi on his mobile. He answered with alacrity. I mumbled a 1960s Bombay film song into the receiver. He replied gobbledygook in Hindi, with a few suitably intonated English words—especially "hospital?," "hospital!" "hospital"—thrown in. When I returned from the toilet, Ravi had bad news for me: our cousin had called. Another cousin had been hit by a car. Oh no, I said. We had to meet both the cousins at a hospital where the first cousin was rushing the second cousin.

Our dates looked suitably concerned. They were nice Danish girls with nice Danish hearts. We looked suitably disappointed. We knew from experience that the fact that Ravi and I did not resemble each other in any way would not be noticeable to them; it seldom is to most people in Denmark.

"Families," said Ravi, the dramatist, unable to resist the temptation to improvise, "that's what happens when you have large, extended families."

The girls nodded in sympathy: they read the newspapers and knew all about immigrants with their large families, all of them cramped into little Denmark. Some other time, I am sure, I said, pulling Ravi away before he over-improvised.

We did not have to disguise the haste with which we left.

A few streets away, we dived into the kind of pub that smart young Danish women never enter. Very few of these have been left standing, but there is one at the corner of Christiansgade and Frederiksvej. Dirty and uninviting from the outside; dark, forbidding and smelly inside. Four middle-aged men on stools at the bar turned around to watch us enter. One man revolved all the way around under his initial impetus and had to try again. Two of them kept staring at us, for this was also the kind of pub that colored men did not enter.

I fetched two Tuborgs—only ordinary Danish beers were on offer—from the counter and joined Ravi at a corner table. It was a dark corner. The two men staring at us from the counter went back to contemplating the mysteries of what was definitely their tenth or twelfth glass of beer.

"No more," I said to Ravi, "I am not going on one of these dates ever again."

"So soon, bastard," drawled Ravi, "you give up so bloody soon. How many have you dated: three, four, five? Look at me, I am on number seventy-nine: I am getting there. Any day now I will strike gold: the one girl out of a hundred in Århus who doesn't date only white men or only colored men. That will be history! Tales will be told of us in the annals of this city. People will rank us with Frederick Douglass and Martin Luther King. Don't throw up your spade, bastard; keep digging.

"Actually," he added, "I was not averse to playing some ball games with Miss Spiky Hair, but the urgency of your weak-kneed knocks made me abandon the idea. What is it that repelled you, O Worshipper of Shallow Beauty, about Miss Monroe in extra size? I thought she was just up your alley and was quite convinced, until you knocked, that you would be up her alley tonight, incurring the sleepless, unspoken wrath of good old Karim Bhai."

"She only dates colored men," I replied.

"Good for her! All the more reason to do your duty: I have never understood what you have against that nineteen percent of the female population here. She likes colored men: good. You are colored: good. So go ahead, bastard, prove to her that you are a fucking man."

"Don't be more facetious than usual, Ravi."

"You know, you bloody wog, you are going the way of all these bloody niggers. There was a time when they came to Europe, flaunted the invisible chains of slavery in the face of white women, hyped up natural rhythm and the animal in man, and merrily spiked the entire lot before white men could even clear their throats to object. White women dangled from their proverbially big dicks, desperate for redemption. Now my nigger friends get all intellectual and sensitive, point out uninteresting facts like the normality of their dicks, and lose white women to, horror of horrors, limpid white men. And it is the same with us wogs: there was a time when we floated around on our magic carpets of mysticism, bestowing our largesse with typical Oriental abundance. Sri Aurobindo had his share of Mas, Nehru netted Edwina, Bapu had a surfeit of admiring blonde Bais, Behns... Then comes our generation, claiming to be rational, doing engineering, computers and medicine; medicine, good lord! Shit, man, what's wrong with us? Why can't we use the few fucking advantages history has left us with?"

Ravi had raised his voice during this harangue, and one of the starers at the counter turned to frown at us. Ravi frowned back.

Medicine was Ravi's weak point. He hated the field with a vengeance. He claimed it had to do with his dad, a legendary Mumbai surgeon, and the final fight that the two of them had when Ravi quit medical college in the third year and started doing a degree in the humanities. The university gold medal he got for his master's in history had been scorned by his father. His subsequent diploma in journalism had not helped either. Or his aspiration to write a novel. Since then, they had only communicated through Ravi's mother, though recently relations had thawed slightly. Ravi's decision—after an abandoned career as a staff reporter and no evidence of a published novel—to do a PhD abroad (though still in history, which is what he was doing in Århus), had been more acceptable to his father.

I knew that the volume of his harangue would increase if he got started on medicine, as would his pugilistic tendency to take any objecting middle-aged man as a stand-in for his father. I steered him gently out of the pub, all four customers at the counter staring at us, and into the streets. They were probably safe now: there was a good chance our ex-dates had gone home.

When we returned to the flat that night, well after midnight, there was a note from Karim on the kitchen table. "Salaam-alai-kum. Night shift today; will be back for breakfast," it said. Karim Bhai was very conscientious. He seldom left the flat without leaving a note for us. He kept a list of "supplies to be bought" hanging from a magnet on the fridge, and diligently crossed items out or added them in his neat handwriting. If he expected something similar from us, he bravely kept his disappointment from showing.

The next morning, I woke up expecting a call from my parents in Karachi. It was Saturday; they called every Saturday morning. I was waiting for the chirr of the phone while taking out cartons of milk and juice from the fridge and toasting bread. The coffee machine gurgled. Ravi was traversing the lobby, wrapped in a towel on his way out of the shower, and he picked up the phone when it rang. I expected him to hand it to me, but he continued talking into the receiver.

It soon became obvious that the caller was not one of my parents. It was someone doing tabligh: trying to preach the virtues of the Quran. Perhaps it was someone known to Karim. Perhaps he thought Ravi was Karim. I had heard of these phonic proselytizers, but never experienced one—and I wondered, for the person evidently spoke Urdu, if the call was not from India or Pakistan. In any case, the number was a secret one; it did not show on our phone.

Talking about the Quran was not an issue for Ravi, but the secrecy of the number perturbed the democratic Indian in him. Between questions and answers about the Quran, of which he probably knew as much as the anonymous proselytizer, Ravi kept querying him about his identity and the need to use a number that did not show.

I signaled to Ravi to cut the connection; I am expecting a call, I mouthed at him. He ignored me and continued to discuss some fine point of Quranic exegesis.

I wrenched the receiver away from him. He would have resisted but for the fact that he was still clad in a precariously knotted towel, which had to be kept in place with one hand.

"Hello, hello," said the voice on the other end. Then it continued in chaste Urdu, "As the Quran Sharif says in its infinite wisdom..."

"Excuse me," I said, in chaste Urdu too, "the connection is extremely bad. I cannot hear you very well."

There was a bit of beeping. The guy evidently had a team working on the technology. Volume and audibility increased.

"Is it better now?" the anonymous proselytizer asked.

"Hello, hello," I replied. "I cannot hear you..."

"Just a second, janaab. Don't put down the phone."

"Hello," I said, "hello, hello, hello..." I put the receiver down.

The phone rang again in two seconds.

I put it down once more with a string of strangulated hellos. Ravi came out of his room, buttoning his jeans, bare-chested.

He shook his head.

"You, my friend, are the reason why the infidels are winning," he said.

After a slow breakfast, he diligently practiced the postures of prayer that Karim Bhai was teaching him. He ignored my comment about it being symbolic compensation for the disappointments of last night.

When we finally left for the university library around noon, Karim Bhai had not returned despite his note of the previous evening.

RETROSPECTIVE MYSTERIES

By three in the afternoon, Ravi had abandoned the library building, ambitiously shaped to resemble a book from the outside, though the resemblance was more imaginary than architectural, and SMS-ed a rendezvous with one of his "plain" girlfriends. Ravi was a restless researcher: this did not show in his work or erudition, which was sustained by a consciously camouflaged ability to read and absorb faster than anyone else I have known. He must have been obnoxious as a school student. I would have hated going to the same class as him, for I came to my education through diligence and perseverance. Ravi tried to make light of this difference on the occasions I brought it up, pointing out the fact that while I was being taught English, Urdu and a faint smattering of French by my Jesuits in Karachi, he was being taught English, Hindi and French by his Jesuits, as well as Sanskrit, Latin, German and the piano by a succession of private tutors employed by his parents.

But it was true. Facts, fiction, languages did not flock to me, without significant effort on my part. They did to Ravi. They were like the "plain" women he dated—some of whom were plain only by the standards of a man who had grown up among Bollywood starlets.

But flock to him they did, despite what Ravi called his "absolute honesty": the fact that he made no promise of fidelity, that he actually promised infidelity and impermanence. I am a postmodern lover, he would clarify; you, bastard, are still stuck knee-deep in modernity.

When I returned to the flat that evening, there were sounds coming from Ravi's room. The rhythm of love-making, communicated by the creaking of his bed, which soon swelled to an unrestrained crescendo of ecstasy in a male and a female voice. I was becoming familiar with these noises, and wondered what Karim Bhai thought of them. There was no sign of Karim Bhai, but I assumed he had called or met Ravi earlier on. I shut myself up in my room with one of the last volumes of my Proust.

An hour later, Ravi knocked on my door, opened it and did a fair imitation of a siren blowing. All clear, bastard, he announced. Let's get a pizza.

Over the pizza, he asked me if Karim Bhai had come back and left again during his moments of ecstasy.

"But I thought you had heard from him," I said.

"No. There was no sign of him." We were somewhat worried.

"Should we call and ask?" wondered Ravi. We had exchanged mobile numbers on moving in. But we decided not to call; it appeared a bit excessive, given the phlegmaticism with which Karim mostly treated events and things.

This was our first month in the flat, and Karim had always appeared to be such a careful, methodical man: we could not help worrying. We were about to call him when, at about nine that night, we heard his cab pull up. Karim Bhai came in and went into his room. He usually kept the door of his room slightly open, even at night, but tonight he closed it firmly. Next morning, he remained reticent about his disappearance, and we saw no cause to press him for information.

In later months, we would get used to such sudden dis-appearances by Karim Bhai. We would not pay it much attention, perhaps even attributing it to the kind of carnal needs that we indulged in, Ravi with far greater abundance than me, and that Karim Bhai appeared to be so unaffected by. Perhaps, I remember thinking, he needs a day or a night out with some prostitute. It made sense to me: I could not imagine a man to whom sex did not matter.

Later on, when the controversy broke over us, we started pondering more about these mysterious disappearances of Karim Bhai. They came to be colored the shade of suspicion that was being cast on all of us by the Danish tabloids. But that was still almost a year off; I should stick to the forgotten injunctions of my girlfriend of yore and keep that story for later. Too much movement back and forth in time, I almost remember her quoting her MFA professor, loses more readers than it gains.

Ravi, who could have easily got a role as a star in any Bollywood film on the basis of his looks alone—not to mention the contacts that his surgeon father and his socialite-actress mother had in that city of connections—never dated girls he did not consider "plain." He had a theory about it, which he had explained many times to me (and once, to her great irritation, to my ex-wife). One evening, with the February Århus sky blanketing all desire to go out, he explained it to Karim. We had been drinking gin—Ravi and I, that is—in his room, where he had installed a small bar with a fridge. While my room was filled with Ikea furniture and Karim's with secondhand stuff bought over a number of years, Ravi's room had an expensive four-poster bed, a small ivory-topped table, a revolving Victorian book rack, and this bar, leaving just enough space to walk from the door to the window at the other end.

Despite his legendary spat with his father, Ravi's mother still sent him hundred-dollar bills in unregistered envelopes—something Karim Bhai was shocked at, for he was afraid the money would be lost in transit and did not realize how small these sums were for Ravi's family. Consequently, Ravi usually had more money than he needed. The bar had been purchased to enable us to drink in his room when Karim Bhai was around. When Karim Bhai was in the flat, for some reason, even though he never forbade it, we never took a drink into the kitchen. We never even entered Karim Bhai's room if we had been drinking, but we would sometimes go to the kitchen for a coffee, and then Karim Bhai, if he was around, joined us and pretended not to notice our slightly inebriated state.

"You see, Karim Bhai," Ravi said that evening in the kitchen, more drunk than usual, "plain girls are the salt of the earth: they do things to you. Beautiful girls expect you to do things to them."

"Do things for you?" Karim Bhai corrected him hesitatingly. He had just handed Ravi one of his carefully rolled cigarettes, after I had declined.

"No, Karim Bhai. To you. You know, they do things to you. They do not just lie under you or straddle you and expect their beauty to do all their work for them. If you want real sex, Karim Bhai, you know, the stuff that sends the world whirring for a minute like a ceiling fan, go for the plain women of the world."

Karim Bhai was already blushing behind his beard. He had the pink complexion of some north Indian men, as did Ravi. I am much darker, and Ravi had on occasions pointed out, given his ironic penchant for stereotypes, that the two of them, despite being "bloody Indians," would pass for any "frontier Pashtun," while I, being "a bloody Paki," disgraced my nationality and looked like a "darkie Hindoo." That's because, Ravi would add, this bastard is not a real Paki; he is a fucking mohajir.

That is true. My grandparents had left India with their children during the partition years. I sometimes meet mohajirs in Pakistan who wax eloquent about all they lost in India and lament the partition. In my case, I am grateful to Jinnah, Patel, Nehru,

Mountbatten, Lady and Lord, whoever it was that fucked up in 1947 and sent millions of people to their graves or across invisible borders. Huge tragedy, sure, don't misread me; but in my case, only good came out of it. I once, just once, visited the town—home, they called it until their death—that my grandparents had left in India. It was a desolate, dingy, dry little landlocked place called Phansa in Bihar. I returned to lovely, vibrant, seaside Karachi, relieved to be a mohajir. Since then, I have always been thankful to the whole blind bickering gang of them for their fuck-ups in 1947.

Ravi was blind to Karim Bhai's blush. When Ravi got going on his theories, especially if he was a bit drunk, he seldom noticed their effects. All of Our Forcibly Shared Great Western Civilization, he once explained, is evidence of the fact that great men are never aware of the effects of their theories on others.

What Ravi claimed was not entirely true. Not all of Ravi's "plain" girls did things "to" him. He himself divided them up into those with whom he had a Platonic relationship, those with whom he had a Gandhian relationship and those who joined him in a Marxist relationship. The Platonic ones were to contemplate and forget; the Gandhian ones were to fumble with, to hug and huddle, but nothing more; the Marxist ones were, as he put it, to screw and get screwed by.

Why Marxist, I had questioned him, for I considered myself more or less a Marxist.

"Because Marx had an illegitimate daughter, O Ignorant Son of the Bourgeoisie, because Engels had a series of mistresses, and, above all, because, as any True Marxist will tell you, history is merely the progress of the classes fucking each other up," he had explained on that occasion.

But even when it came to his Marxist relationships, Ravi sometimes encountered women who either did not do things "to" him or who withdrew their initiative unexpectedly. At first, I had expected Ravi to take these setbacks in his stride; after all, it was seldom that he was not dating, openly and unabashedly, at least two women. And he did take them well, but not without a lurch. I knew one of his girlfriends had broken up with him unexpectedly, or vice versa, when Ravi would requisition me and march us to the nearest bar; he would proceed to get so drunk that I had to tuck him into his bed that night.

The last week of February was a particularly remarkable one on these counts. On Thursday, Ravi broke it off with one of the three women he was having his cultural revolutions with at the time.

"She is getting too emotional, you know, yaar," he explained to me. "A bit like one of your purdah-shrouded khatoons probably got with you in Pakistan."

"You don't know what you are talking about, Ravi," I countered. "Have you ever crossed the gates of any of those Muslim girls' colleges? The kind of comments our gals in purdah aim at a good-looking man would drive any civilized Paleface to turn reddish Indian and scalp himself."

"Anyway, yaar: not part of the deal. I cannot be responsible for emotions; I love these women, but I don't think I can love anyone forever."

This was one of Ravi's refrains. I had come to suspect, through occasional lapses on his part—for Ravi was unusually secretive about these matters—that this had to do with his parents' marriage. There was a kind of cynicism in Ravi that either denoted too much knowledge or too much innocence. Only much later did I realize that it could denote both.

Having broken off with Ms. Emotional that Thursday evening—it is not something Ravi did without remorse—he was given his marching slips by the other two girlfriends on Friday.

When I finished teaching around two that afternoon, I had a text message waiting on my mobile. It was from Ravi. "Need to drown hat-trick in hooch," it said. "Meet at Unibar 1600."

Unibar is Århus University's only half-hearted attempt to exorcize the ghost of Denmark's Calvinist past that occasionally stalks the land even today. University canteens close by four, and the campus area doesn't have any decent bar or pub, something that Ravi found impossible to reconcile with his idea of campus life.

Even I, growing up in the more austere environment of post-Zia Pakistan, was used to cafés and restaurants that stayed open and crowded with students late into the night: what could be drunk was only tea, coffee or lassi, but it was drunk with gusto and the debates and arguments did not suffer from the lack of openly served alcohol.

Such places do not seem to exist on Danish campuses, though there are occasional Friday night bars organized by students here and there, where loud music and cheap alcohol make conversation impossible. Unibar, tucked into the basement of a building in the campus, is an exception: not only does it stay open well beyond midnight, it even stocks one of the best collections in town of Ravi's beloved German and Belgian beers and plays (good) music softly enough to permit conversation.

Ravi was already into his second Chimay—2009, he liked to move back from the most recent year—beer when I joined him. He took his break-ups quite seriously, one of the things that was surprising and endearing about him, at least in my eyes. He appeared almost disappointed in himself and the world every time one of his relationships—invariably proclaimed impermanent by him—actually failed. For an evening or two, he did a fairly good imitation of Rajesh Khanna or Dilip Kumar in one of their tearjerkers, sometimes even singing songs of heartbreak in his mellifluous voice, with just enough irony in the rendition to prevent one from taking him too seriously. Then he bounced back and was off dating another "plain" woman.

"Why don't you date only one at a time?" I asked him that evening. "You would avoid these double and triple whammies in that case."

By then Ravi was on to Chimay 2007.

"I am being kind to them, O Dense One," he replied. "If I date only one, she is liable to invest more in the relationship, and anyone who invests in relationships is heading for bankruptcy."

"But why, Ravi," I pressed the matter, mostly to humor him. "Why are all relationships doomed in advance?"

"Look who is talking. Dr. Once-divorced-and-still-bindaas!" Ravi sneered.

Then he sobered up a bit, probably realizing that he had gone too far. My divorce had not been a flippant matter for me or my ex-wife.

"Did I tell you, bastard," he continued, "about my years in Switzerland?"

"I know you finished your high school in Switzerland. You told me your parents sent you there for three years or so."

"Did I tell you why?"

"I don't recall if you did."

"Oh, you would, if I had told you. It is an unforgettable story, the kind of story that gets made into TV serials five times a day. See, bastard, you obviously did not peruse Indian film magazines in high school. I wonder what you used to jerk off to, probably Billy Shakespeare: cabin'd, cribb'd, confined in Karachi, bound to saucy fears... Now, if you had employed your time fruitfully with Cineblitz, Filmfare and the like, you would have read in their issues of the 1980s and early 1990s about this very handsome celebrity Bombay surgeon who was having a roaring affair with one of his star patients, a famous actress. They carried something about it in almost every issue. It was good for circulation. You might also have read of this celebrity surgeon's wife, herself a once-celebrated actress and socialite, being seen on the arms of various film stars and cricketers, including the great Imran, in the same period. There were rumors of impending divorce. I was sent to Switzerland when the rumors were at their height. When I returned, hallelujah, the rumors had evaporated."

He took a deep draft from his glass, draining it. Then he got up to fetch himself Chimay 2006. Before he left the table, he added, as if to himself, "But, strangely, only the rumors had disappeared."

"Why do you call each other 'bastards'?" Karim Bhai asked us one day. "It is not a nice word, you know."

"We went to a missionary school, Karim Bhai," Ravi responded.

"Not the same one, true. In two different countries, yes. Enemy nations even. But Jesuit schools, so it hardly mattered."

Karim Bhai, who had been educated in government schools, did not get the joke.

"Immaculate conception, Karim Bhai," Ravi explained. "There is no greater term of honor than bastard in those circles."

Karim Bhai still did not understand. But Ravi had moved onto other topics. Which was just as well, I thought; it was obvious that Karim Bhai took Jesus—Isa Masih to him—very seriously as a prophet who was destined to return and restore the world to Islam and righteousness.

It had by now become clear to us that we had underestimated Karim Bhai's religiosity. His flat was a hub for informal Quranic studies every Friday evening, when young men, mostly bearded, and women, mostly shrouded, would descend on it for long discussions over coffee, tea, nimki and other snacks that Karim diligently stocked. These ended at nine sharp, when Karim went off to ply his taxi, unwilling to let religion deprive him of the lucrative Friday-night custom.

In the first few weeks, we had missed these sessions. We had hit town early on those Friday evenings. But when Ravi discovered the sessions, he started making a conscious effort to attend them. I would either stay in my room or go out with friends. Sometimes he would join us much later in the night.

Once I ribbed him about it. I did not understand his interest in such sessions.

"You underestimate them, bastard," he replied. "They are far more pertinent and political than almost all the academic seminars that I have attended. They discuss matters of significance and do it honestly: how to make sense of the world, how to make it a better world. They still have a conscience, these young men and women, not just a bank account like the rest of these people."

He waved his hand at the young people drinking and dancing in the Irish pub we were in.

"I know all about the politics," I retorted. "I grew up with politics beating down on me. Basically, it all boils down to three points: the Quran is the final hand-autographed word of God; the West is fucking us; the Jews are fucking us via the West."

"You know, bastard, that I would not let that kind of racism go unchallenged. Actually, while they are probably very anti-Israel, they do not really discuss the matter much."

"Yes, because you are there."

"Listen to yourself, yaar. You sound like a Danish tabloid. What do you think they are? The secret Århus cell of Al Qaeda?"

"Who knows?"

"Karim Bhai, a terrorist! Really, have you ever come across a person with more seriousness of purpose, more consideration for other people's space, you fanatic? He lets us drink in his flat, and you know what alcohol means to people like him."

"Perhaps he needs the money more than he hates alcohol."

"Oh yes, perhaps he is the main funder of Al Qaeda? That's why he needs the money so badly!"

"Who knows? He works all the time; he disappears suddenly; he gets strange phone calls; you cannot deny he needs the money for some reason."

"The same reason as all immigrants except fucking privileged ones like us. He probably sends money home to his family. You know, bastard, you have been in the West too long; go back home. You need a shot of sanity."

"Sanity was banned in Pakistan by Zia, bastard," I replied. "And that is one ban no one is going to lift."

But Ravi was right. I was arguing just to irk him. I did not really suspect Karim of being a radical Islamist, let alone a terrorist. Not yet.

I think it was soon after this conversation that Ravi started growing a beard: a stylish, French-cut beard, but still. "Don't tell me Karim Bhai has converted you," I remarked to him. "It is an experiment, bastard," he replied mysteriously.

Karim's days were patterned. He worked as many shifts as he could. It was Friday afternoons and evenings that he kept free: for his weekly trip to the mosque, which was a room in a private house, and for his Quranic sessions. When he was not working, he was usually home, reading some commentary on the Quran, praying, telling his blue-speckled-with-black beads or watching TV in his room. He would tidy up regularly, even offering to tidy up in our rooms if we were around. Cleanliness was a mantra with him. He was not too orderly, though, leaving things lying about as long as they were not dirty.

Once in a while, his routine existence would be disturbed by a phone call. Looking back, when suspicion gripped me towards the end of our stay in Karim's flat, I identified two kinds of phone calls. Most of them were the normal kind: Karim would pick up the phone and talk into the receiver, in Danish, English or Urdu, about various mundane matters. If one of us picked up the phone, there would be a voice at the other end identifying himself or (very rarely) herself and asking for Karim. Then there were the usual wrong numbers. Perhaps too many, I suspected later on, though some of them—like the woman who called asking, in slurred Danish, to be connected to her "mand," or the child who dialed incorrectly— seemed innocuous enough.

But the second kind of phone call was different and much rarer. So rare that we paid it sufficient attention only in retrospect, when suspicion left us with no choice. The phone would ring. If Ravi or I picked it up, sometimes it would go dead. It would ring again, and usually Karim Bhai would pick it up with alacrity if he was in the flat. If he wasn't, it might go dead again and not ring for the next six hours, which was the usual duration of Karim Bhai's shifts. When Karim Bhai picked up the phone, his conversation was restrained, seldom going beyond yes or no. Once I heard him say in Danish, in a tone of irritation, "Why do you always forget to call me on my mobile?" Though he was immediately contrite after that. He started apologizing, but then the phone went dead. A few seconds later Karim Bhai got a call on his mobile, which he answered in his room after, unusually, closing the door.

All this went unremarked by me then, as did the young men and (fewer) women who came to Karim Bhai's Friday sessions. Later, when I mentioned these calls to the police, the interrogating officer looked visibly pleased. He was less pleased by my inability to give him a full description of most of the young men and women.

But, like the phone calls, I had not noticed them then. If I had noticed them, I had noticed the resemblance between them: beards and veils.

On faces of different colors—mostly South Asian, occasionally European, African, or Indonesian- or Malaysian-looking—but framed by the same seriousness of purpose, the same solemnity, the same sparse or full growth of hair on their chins, the same wrap of cloth around their head... I could not have described them if I had wanted to. The only one I could have described was Ali. Or Ajsa. But of course, the police knew all about Ali and Ajsa by then. And, to be honest, Ajsa, as far as Ravi and I could recall, had attended only one of the sessions.

It had been a morning in March. I am certain about that because, after relenting in February, the cold had returned with a vengeance so that, when the bell rang and I opened the door, the chill cut me to the bone, although the flat was on the third floor. Standing outside, all wrapped up, with just some wisps of her blonde hair showing, was a young woman. For a moment I thought she was one of Ravi's new girlfriends, but she was by no means "plain," even by Ravi's standards. A tall, willowy woman, blue-eyed, blonde, almost my height: she was evidently Danish. I was surprised when she asked for Karim Bhai. She called him "bhai" too, which was just as surprising.

As Karim had been on a night shift and was expected to return any moment, and as we were going to have breakfast in the kitchen, I asked her to join us. She did, though just for a coffee. When I introduced her to Ravi, she looked unsurprised—both by his looks, which seldom went unnoticed, and by his presence.

"It is good to meet both of you," she said. "Karim Bhai was so happy when you rented the rooms after Babo and Mama vacated

31

in such a huff. He was uncertain he would be able to rent out the rooms again, at least not both of them. You know how Danes are."

It was then that we understood who she was. She was not Danish. She was the young Bosnian woman whose elopement with a religious Somali man had cost Karim Bhai his previous tenants. She introduced herself as Ajsa and kept out of our conversation, absentmindedly sipping from the mug that I had handed her. I could now see that she had a smart veil wrapped around her blonde hair. It was there for propriety, not to keep out the cold.

She spoke a bit more when Karim Bhai came in and joined us for breakfast. It was mostly about her husband. Much of it was too cryptic for me to follow, but I could sense that she was worried about the Somali. His name, I gathered, was Ibrahim. I remember that towards the end of the conversation, she said:

"You know how Ibrahim feels about the cartoons. You know how he is."

At this, Karim Bhai said to her, glancing surreptitiously at us, "Perhaps we can talk about it some other time. I will call on both of you."

I knew he could not take Ajsa to his room: his understanding of his religion prohibited him from being alone in a room with her, and for all I knew, she shared those values too. She was a young woman who had discovered Islam as a reaction to both her parents and the place that history had confined her to: a place where her Nordic looks would probably efface her more easily than if she had been dark-haired and dark-eyed. But it was also obvious that they wanted to talk about matters without Ravi or me overhearing.

Until the events that put things in perspective, whenever Ajsa came to call on Karim Bhai, I sensed the same hesitation and secrecy. I mentioned this to the police officer later on. He smiled grimly and nodded.

GREAT CLAUS AND LITTLE CLAUS

There is a poem by Henrik Nordbrandt, the only Danish poet Ravi, whose conversations were otherwise peppered with quotations from Hindi, English, French, German and, especially, carefully enunciated Urdu poems, ever quoted in my hearing. It lists the months of the Danish year as being thirteen: "januar, februar, marts, april, maj, juni, juli, august, september, oktober, november, november, november."

November had lasted, with a short break in February, well into March now, extending the Danish year by another two dark, blowsy, wet, cold months. Though the snow had melted, once in a while the air still filled with white flakes, making me feel as if I was trapped inside one of those paperweights that, in the heat of Karachi, had once looked so tempting. You know, the ones with white fluff swimming in the water: you shake them and it snows all over the plastic Alps or some pretty European cut-out village inside the glass.

Perhaps it was the weather that kept us indoors more often than not during the daytime. In Ravi's case, it might also have been the PhD thesis or, what was more likely, the novel that he was working on. He preferred writing at home. I would go out more often, as I had to teach and attend the usual interminable departmental meetings, where we pretended to be democratic even as all significant decisions were increasingly made way above us. But on days when there was no teaching, I would loiter in the flat too, reading, instead of following my usual routine and going to the library. Very soon, we learned to place the other residents of the building.

Divided by a winding central staircase, with frail-looking wooden railings, the building rose to five stories. It was a pre-war construction. On both sides of the staircase, past the narrow-latticed landing, there were two-bedroom flats exactly like Karim Bhai's. Most of them were occupied by young couples intending to have a baby and then move out. One couple had a baby of six months. They spent their weekends looking at houses in the suburbs. Ravi was curious about what they would do with their weekends once they actually bought their suburban house. A couple of the flats were rented by university students: two men in one and three women in the other. Only the top two flats contained anyone even as old as Karim Bhai.

The top two flats had been converted into one spacious flat by the family that lived there and, according to Karim, had lived there for almost two decades. The father, Claus, was a doctor, and the mother, Pernille, was a secretary at the university. Both were in their early fifties. Their twin daughters had moved out just a year ago when they started attending university.

Though Karim Bhai knew everyone who lived in the flats by name—we later realized that many of them booked his taxi in the black—he visited and was visited by only Claus and Pernille. This might have been due to their age. Karim Bhai found it easier to talk to people who were a decade older than him than to people who were a decade younger. But there were other factors too.

Pernille and particularly Claus took a sort of fraternal interest in Karim Bhai and, by extension, us. Claus had seen us moving our furniture and cartons up on the very first day and had offered to help. When we had declined, he had dropped in the next evening with Pernille and greeted us with a resonant salaam-alai-kum. He had followed this up with a heavily accented "sob kuch teek-taak, na?," his small grey eyes twinkling impishly. It turned out that he had spent a number of months in Pakistan, working for various NGOs, mostly "Læger Uden Grænser," Doctors Without Borders. Claus was a large, bearded man beside whom the shrunken, skinny Pernille looked even smaller.

It soon became clear to us that Claus was used to dropping in for a chat every third day or so. With Karim Bhai, and now us, he assumed a persona that was consciously pruned of Danish constraint. Pernille was a more rare and reserved visitor. Usually Claus would drop in with his friend, also a doctor, whose name was Hans. Hans was a slightly smaller version of Claus, and Ravi soon dubbed him Little Claus. Bearded, broad and only a couple of inches under Great Claus's six feet, the friends could have passed for lumberjacks. Or surgeons, Ravi corrected me. Surgeons look like lumberjacks, he added.

Little Claus had also spent time in Pakistan. Actually, it turned out that, from the time the two met in the third year of their medical studies at Copenhagen, Great and Little Claus had gone on regular NGO trips to various parts of Asia and Africa, taking some months off every couple of years or so. It is our idea of a vacation, they had explained modestly. Pernille, whose interest in the world was less pronounced and whose career was tied to daily working hours, had mostly stayed home with the kids on these occasions. Perhaps she had resented it but realized too late; perhaps, like other people of her generation and class, she would have liked living in a suburban house instead of a double-flat that fitted Claus's peripatetic lifestyle. But these doubts came to me only much later.

There was a soft knock. It was a Thursday afternoon. I was in my room; Ravi was banging away at his laptop in the kitchen; Karim was out on one of his shifts.

One of the two Clauses, I said to Ravi. They were the only people who knocked instead of ringing the bell.

"Great Claus, Elementary Watson," Ravi commented. "Great Claus has a little knock; Little Claus has a great knock." Both the Clauses were there, with a cake.

"Sob kuch teek-taak, na?" said Great Claus. It had become his standard greeting with us. Having realized that Ravi was a Hindu and I was a ham-eating, wine-drinking Muslim, he had reserved his resonant "salaam-alai-kum" for Karim.

"Where is Karim?" he said now. "We have a cake for him, made personally by moi with strictly halal ingredients."

"It is Claus's birthday," Little Claus explained.

They were disappointed when they heard that Karim was out. Then Great Claus cheered up. Wait a sec, he said and ran upstairs. He was back in a minute with a bottle of champagne and four glasses.

"We can keep the cake for Karim and celebrate with something less Islamic," he announced, pouring the bubbly into glasses in the kitchen.

"Shouldn't you be celebrating with your family?" I said.

"I will; I will; I am a bleddy good familiefar," replied Great Claus with just a hint of bitterness.

We toasted him.

"Skål!" said Little Claus, lastly, "to our twentieth, Claus, min ven!"

Great Claus looked visibly touched. There were tears in his eyes. Perhaps that's why he needed to explain the toast to us.

"You see," he said, "this is the twentieth birthday that I have celebrated with Hans here or in Pakistan or in Kenya..."

Little Claus looked pensive.

"I have celebrated more birthdays with you, min ven, than I have with anyone else," added Great Claus, laying his slightly bigger hand on Little Claus's paw.

Hold nu op, retorted Little Claus with gruff affection. Then both of them looked embarrassed and switched the topic to the political situation in Libya.

The phone rang a few minutes after the two Clauses had left, carrying the bottle and glasses back with them. I picked it up. It was a woman's voice, asking for Karim. It sounded very Danish. I replied that Karim was not back yet from his shift.

The woman repeated her question, as if she had not heard me. Can I... can I speak to Karim, she said in Danish.

As my Danish is far from perfect and Ravi speaks the language with flourish, I handed the receiver to him. He repeated what I had said in an accent that, I was convinced, would have been easy to follow even for a Dane living in some remote fishing village off the coasts of Jutland.

But I could hear that the woman did not understand.

"I want to speak to Karim," she almost sobbed.

Then, as Ravi started to repeat his answer, she disconnected the line.

Once, the two Clauses knocked on a Friday evening, just before Karim's Quranic session was to begin. Usually Karim turned people away during these sessions, unless they were part of his discussion group. But he let the Clauses in. It indicated to me how close he felt to these two bearded men who had spent most of their vacations treating poor people in remote villages of Asia and Africa.

But when Great Claus wanted to hold the Quran—in Arabic, Urdu and English—that Karim passed around and referred to, Karim apologetically pulled it away. "It is a holy book, Claus, if I may," he said in Danish. "You should be clean before you can hold it."

It was then that I realized, for the first time, that Karim had never let me or Ravi touch his Quran either. Ravi because he was, despite his interest in the religion, not a Muslim and me because, in Karim Bhai's eyes, I had sullied myself with alcohol, non-halal food and probably—he was right in suspecting—I did not perform the ritual stinja cleansing every time I pissed.

That night the two Clauses joined Ravi and me on our regular Friday night out in town. We did not have a date that Friday. We had just decided to meet some friends from the university in a café. Little Claus and Great Claus spent much of the time huddled together, talking. I overheard them discussing Great Claus's family. At one point, Great Claus sounded irritated, and Little Claus left the table to get himself another drink from the bar.

Great Claus followed him with his beer. He put a reassuring bear-arm around Little Claus's shoulders at the bar. The two friends stood there talking for half an hour. When we decided to move to another café, the Clauses said they would be heading home soon and stayed back.

My last sight of them that night was of two large men, both bearded, bent over their beers at the bar, conversing with a quiet intensity that is rare to observe in these parts.

LILACS OUT OF THE DEAD LAND

It had been a cold March, but April showed promise. Branches let out shoots, though still curled into themselves, chary of the chill; the sky brightened and appeared to expand a bit with the light; one could even hear birds twittering. Ravi ploughed into his PhD thesis, which was long due now, having finally abandoned the third novel that he had started since the days he quit medical studies. He had a literary reputation in India and UK: he had been anthologized by Pankaj Mishra and mentioned as "a name to watch" by Salman Rushdie, an unusual combination, almost a decade ago, and a year back he had contributed to a special number of *Granta*. For more than a decade, he had been rumored to be the next Vikram Seth, perhaps even the next Arundhati Roy, gender permitting. Unfortunately, he had never managed to finish a novel or a full collection of any sort. His reputation would wax and wane with a brilliant story here, a cutting essay there.

Still, it was an international literary reputation, if only in select circles, and I never understood why my department did not invite him for readings or talks. I had offered to set one up for him, but Ravi did not want the invitation to proceed from me. My

39

colleagues, whenever I mentioned him, made appreciative noises; they did not send him an invitation.

Ravi had his explanation: "Almost all the tenured Brits and Yankees in English departments in Denmark, who are basically there because they are Americans and Brits, and all the Danes, who are there because they are Danes, which makes better sense to me, love multicultural literature, bastard. You know they do. We know they do. It reminds them of their great-grandparents in the colonies. Of course, they love Rushdie and Naipaul. Naipaul, Kureishi, Rushdie: why, these guys are so Indian they even speak with an English accent! That's why people like us should write novels, yaar; imagine your colleagues wriggling in their desire to be open and their subterranean terror of us pilfering their bread-and-butter tongue, and that too in our consciously roti-and-ghee accent."

Ravi never understood why I did not write creatively. For him, literature was an art. He often forgot that for a middle-class family like mine, it was primarily a profession. I taught English literature because I had not been good enough to get into any major medical or engineering college and my parents, university lecturers themselves (though in physics and sociology), could not afford to buy me an education. I was good enough for the less competitive humanities. I could earn a scholarship to England.

Ravi was too privileged, and education came too easily to him; he could not imagine educating himself for merely a profession. He had once told me that his father still invested in shares and bank certificates—"for tax reasons, you know, bastard"—in his name, so that he had a couple of millions waiting for him, no matter what happened. That he did not draw on them was part of his protest against his parents. But he knew the millions were there, stashed away, gathering interest or appreciating, and he was honest enough to concede that he did not feel the need to slog for a salary.

Ravi was driven by ideals that he scoffed at in public. He was driven by dreams he was openly skeptical of. He hacked his own pathways, sometimes—I felt—at the risk of slicing off a part of himself. His PhD thesis was taking longer than it should have simply because he was no longer overly interested in it. Once he had worked an idea out in his mind, Ravi seldom saw the need to continue to write it down.

He had started working on the history of fascism and Nazism in Denmark. He could be acerbic about it: "They tell you the moment you set foot here that they managed to smuggle all the Jews out of Denmark when the Nazis wanted to round them up. They forget to mention that it was a German officer who leaked the Nazis' plans to the Danish resistance, which was largely communist and outlawed by the Danish government. They forget to tell you that the only people, apart from the poor fucking Germans, to form a full SS regiment were the good blue-eyed Danes!"

But the thesis, like most PhDs, had changed direction over the years. Now it was a more theoretical study in which, Ravi claimed, he was tracing the links between fascism and North European notions of order. "Fascism," he would declaim over a few drinks, "is above all the ideology of order."

"Exclusive order, you mean?" I had once queried.

"There is no such thing, bastard," he had replied. "You either have order or you have shades of disorder. All order is essentially exclusive; it does not have degrees, like disorder. You can have order only by eliminating. Elimination is its essence. All order has genocide hidden in its belly. Give it nine months and it will give birth, under clement conditions of course, to a holocaust."

It was difficult to tell with Ravi's theories. The ones that he proffered seriously could be the ones he held lightly, or vice versa. But the promise of spring in April was to test one of Ravi's most commonly espoused theories, about plain women. Was Ravi's theory falsifiable? Would it have satisfied Popper?

Because it was to be falsified soon. This is how it happened.

We had been out on our third, and last, double date. This time it appeared to be going well. We had met the women in Under Masken. My date was a German exchange scholar in biology, an attractive woman in her thirties. But the moment we shook hands and sat down, both of us knew that we would not go to bed with each other. We liked each other, it was not that. There was something else, something you come to recognize with time and experience—of which there was sufficient on both sides. You meet someone on a date, you like her, she likes you, and what you feel is a friendship brewing, not romance. When you are young or desperate, you ignore that feeling and spoil what could have been a beautiful friendship. But my date and I were neither too young nor too desperate; we recognized the feeling in each other and we respected it. It led to a pleasant evening of conversation. Neither of us contemplated taking it any further. After about half an hour in Under Masken, we left for another place, as my German date was not a smoker and did not like the smoky atmosphere of the pub.

We left Ravi with his date, a rather pretty—though evidently plain in Ravi's eyes—Turkish woman, who had grown up in Denmark. They appeared to be conversing intently in Danish. Unlike me, Ravi, thanks partly to his prior knowledge of German, spoke the language with near-native fluency. He waved perfunctorily at us when we left. But an hour later, I got a SMS from him: "Collimate Unibar when done with your Deutsch. ☺ " I was not "done with my Deutsch" until after ten, and as mobiles often do not function in the basement where Unibar is tucked away—to avoid affronting the lurking, invisible Calvinist in Danes, Ravi always claimed—I decided to pop in and check on my way back to

Karim Bhai's flat. Ravi was not there. He was not in Karim Bhai's flat either. By midnight, when I went to bed, he had still not returned. I think I heard him return at three or four that night.

Karim Bhai had left for his shift when I woke up around nine and started brewing coffee. Karim Bhai only drank tea, made the Indian way with tea leaves, water, milk, sugar and a dash of cinnamon boiled together in a pan, so the coffee machine was for our use. This was lucky for us, as Karim Bhai sometimes left very early and the coffee machine made a hell of a noise.

Perhaps it was the noise that woke Ravi. Or perhaps he had already been awake, for he came out looking less bleary-eyed than he usually did in the mornings.

"Toast?" I asked him, as he poured himself a cup of coffee.

He shook his head and sat down opposite me at the small kitchen table, cupping his mug and looking into it.

"Hangover?" I asked.

He shook his head again, gazing intently into his future in the coffee cup.

"When did you come in?"

"Around three, I think."

"What happened?" I asked. "You weren't at Unibar."

"I was there until about ten. I fell in with some people I know, PhD students and suchlike."

"I reached the place a bit later," I explained. I wanted to add "you could have SMS-ed." But that sounded like needless nagging, the sort of thing one says to a partner, not to a friend.

Ravi kept staring into his cup.

Then he looked up and his face creased into a brilliant smile.

"You know, bastard, I think I fell in love," he said, and shook his head in wonderment.

Ravi explained that his date with the Turkish woman had been promising, despite the fact that she spoke almost entirely in slang, until she started complaining about immigrants. The core of her complaint was that immigrant men make gross passes at Danish women. Ravi, the Defender of Minorities of All Ilk, could not let that go unchallenged. He argued that all heteromen show interest in women, and many men make passes; the reason why immigrant men become more obvious in a place like Denmark has to do with a certain failure to read signals on all sides. "I can show my interest in Danish women without them getting offended because, thanks to my colonial brainwashing, I do it the way it is sanctioned in Danish society," he claimed, and proceeded to illustrate this with examples. She countered with examples. He deconstructed her examples with increasing relish. She looked irritated. Ravi finally told her to read Fanon, try not to speak so much slang, as she did not need to prove how "well-integrated" she was, and left.

"I don't know what is worse," he said to me, sipping his coffee, "a white woman trying to be colorful or a colored woman trying to be white!"

That was when he had headed for Unibar, where he met a group of PhD students and junior teachers who had been attending a cross-disciplinary conference—"Music and Literature: National Notes, Global Resonances"—and had ended up in the bar too. He had been having a nice time, planning to hang on until I joined him.

"But then," he said, looking at me with a crooked smile, "she walked in."

"Who?"

"Lena."

Lena, spelled the Swedish way with an "a," not an "e," Ravi clarified, as if it was a matter of vital significance, was one of the participants at the conference. She was doing her PhD in musicology but she was also a professional singer, the lead voice in a local jazz band, and a trained opera artiste.

"Don't laugh, bastard," Ravi continued. "This sounds like a cliché. It is a cliché. You know, here I am, in a crowd of men and women, and she walks in. Suddenly the fucking room empties. All I see is her, and I think, where has she been all these years? And, you know, bastard, she comes up to join us and I see her look at me with her green-green eyes, just for a second, you know, just a second; it is a look that speaks to me, it speaks clearly as words; I know, I know that she is thinking exactly the same thing, that the only person she can really see in that fucking crowded room is me."

I might have smiled if it had been anyone other than Ravi: Ravi, who did not believe in love at first sight, Ravi who did not believe in relationships that could last.

"So, what did you do, Great Casanova?" I asked. He gave me his crooked smile again.

"Not me," he replied, "we. We hung around for twenty minutes, pretending to pay attention to the others. Then we started talking only to each other and drifted away from the table. Don't smile, bastard: it wasn't planned. She knew a bit about me, had even read my story in the Mishra anthology. She told me a bit about herself... We ended up walking and talking and then sitting in a café and talking a bit more until, suddenly, it was three. Both of us thought it was only around midnight. I am sorry, I would have SMS-ed you if I had realized how late it was getting..."

"And, and..." I encouraged him, buttering my toast.

"Nothing, bastard. She went home; I came back."

"That is unusual for you, isn't it, Don Juan? Expect me to believe that? I have seen you with women and women with you..."

"This is different, you vulgar Paki," he said.

"Why?" I asked him. "Is she much too plain for your honor?"

"No, bastard," he replied, and he meant it, "she is too fucking beautiful."

He stroked his newly cultivated French beard thoughtfully.

At that moment, the phone rang in the lobby. I went to pick it up. It was the woman who would call on occasion and ask for Karim; I am sure it was the same woman who had not understood me the last time she had called, and had even failed at first to understand Ravi's beautifully intoned Danish. But this time she must have understood my Danish response: Karim er på arbejde. Karim is out working. She disconnected the line immediately. I remember thinking with a smile, surely Karim fulfills his carnal needs despite his Islamic halo!

When I returned to the kitchen, Ravi refused to be drawn back to the topic of Lena. I left soon; I had an appointment with a research student and planned to spend some time after that in the library.

It was one of those days when the wet coldness of late winter turns crisp and you can glimpse the sun behind a thin screen of white clouds. Light fills the land. The bare grey trees, with just a trace of green here and there, fill with diffused sunshine. It is a great time to go out for walks, properly wrapped up, of course, for it is still a cold light that falls from the skies, and the wind, when it blows, can carry shivering tales from the ice further north.

I decided to walk back all the way from the library building to Karim's flat. I reached it well after seven in the evening; I could see that Ravi's sports cycle was not parked outside. Ravi was a cycling enthusiast (I wonder: Do you still cycle now, Ravi? Can you?). The only times he did not use his cycle was when there was a storm or when he had to go out with me, because I do not cycle. He often claimed that the orderly cycle lanes in Denmark were the only redeeming feature of the country's obsession with control and order.

Inside, there was a note on the kitchen table in Ravi's scrawl, signed with an elaborate paraph. It said: "Enjoy your solitude, O Researcher of Literary Superficialities. Karim Bhai rang to annunciate his hegira on 'urgent business,' may Al Qaeda plague you with nightmares, O Apostate; and I am aaf to Lundhun for a hafta or two..."

There are cheap Ryan Air flights to London from Århus's airport as well as neighboring Billund: they usually cost less than a train ticket to Copenhagen. Ravi availed of them on a regular basis, sometimes for seminars or literary readings, and sometimes—always on the spur of the moment—to see a play or just visit friends and buy spices for his cooking. Unlike me, he did not have to teach regularly.

Karim was away for longer than usual. He was away for two nights. When he came back, he looked visibly drained. His face was paler, his short thinning hair and lush greying beard in unusual disarray. But, as always, he did not want to say anything about what he had done and where he had been.

I do not mean to make this sound as suspicious as it does when I write it down here. It is important to explain this, though I am sure my MFA-girlfriend had strictures against such explanations. In any case, I am not writing a novel. This is an account of events that you have read about. And it is necessary to explain that when Karim Bhai returned after two nights, tired and red-eyed, I did not feel suspicious then. Or not suspicious along those lines; I just suspected him of moral double standards. The darker suspicions came only later, when other events overtook us.

One evening Great Claus and Little Claus dropped by as they often did. I remember this was in the week when Ravi was away.

Karim Bhai was home by then. He bustled about the kitchen, brewing chai for his guests. The two Clauses always had tea the Indian way; I think it was one of the things that endeared them to Karim, along with their broken attempts at Urdu.

Great Claus lit his pipe. He knew that Karim Bhai, a regular smoker, would not mind. Little Claus did not smoke, but he had obviously got used to inhaling Great Claus's fumes over the years.

Great Claus's hands shook slightly, as if he was in a state of suppressed excitement. He recounted some tale from his hospital and then the two, old-fashioned social democrats to the core of their hearts, launched into one of their regular critiques: how, over the years, Danish governments had been cutting down on Denmark's public health system in the name of streamlining and at the same time effectively subsidizing private hospitals.

Karim Bhai listened and nodded. He did not participate in the critique. It was then that I realized how, unlike Ravi and, to a lesser extent, myself, Karim Bhai never criticized Denmark. He listened to the criticism with a smile at times, combing his fingers thoughtfully (or craftily? That alternative struck me much later) through his flowing beard. He added a few bits of fact or asked a question. He agreed with the criticism in most cases. But he never said anything critical himself.

I wondered whether it was because he did not trust any of us. Was he more unguarded with his Quranic discussion group when we were not around? Or was it because he did not really care, having given up on Denmark as the land of infidels? The criticism that Ravi or the two Clauses aired was, in different ways, based on a participation in some aspects of life and thinking which was shared by other Danes too. Did Karim Bhai dismiss Denmark to the extent that he felt no need to criticize it?

There was a knock on the door that night, well after eleven. Karim Bhai had fallen asleep, so I opened the door. I had known from the knock that it would be Great Claus. But I was not prepared to find him standing outside in his pajamas, clutching a pillow and with blankets draped all over him.

"Did I wake you up?" he whispered to me.

"I was reading," I replied.

He slid into the lobby, still whispering.

"Can I sleep in Ravi's room tonight?" he asked. He knew that Ravi was in London. "There are guests at our place. I will disappear in the morning."

I was surprised. I had not heard the sound of visitors tramping up the wooden stairs, and it would have taken a horde to make Claus and Pernille run out of beds: they had two extra bedrooms, with their twin daughters having moved out, and a large futon in their sitting room. But I saw no reason to refuse.

Great Claus disappeared sheepishly, blankets trailing behind him, into Ravi's room and carefully closed the door. When I woke up the next morning, the door to Ravi's room was slightly ajar and Great Claus had left. There was a note on the kitchen table, thanking Karim, me and even Ravi, in absentia, and promising us a "pucca mughlai dinner soon as thanks for your garrib-nayvaizzi."

When Ravi returned from London, the first thing he did—after stuffing the larder and the freezer with the Indian ingredients that filled most of his suitcase—was to shut himself up in the toilet. He came out fifteen minutes later, looking a bit different.

He had shaved off the French-style beard that he had grown over the past few weeks.

"What happened, bastard?" I asked him. "Lost your faith so soon?"

"Experiment successfully completed," he replied.

It turned out that his beard had been the outgrowth of Karim Bhai's Quranic sessions but in a typically idiosyncratic way. Indiosyncratic way, Ravi would have said. He had grown it to find out if, as claimed by some of Karim Bhai's fellow-believers, a beard on a Middle Eastern-type face impeded progress through Customs in European airports. Having flown to London, and then to Amsterdam, and from there back to Århus, via Copenhagen—his trajectory over the past week of travels and visits—he had put the hypothesis to test.

"So?" I asked him.

"So what?"

"So, did your beard impede your progress?"

"By an average of two minutes and seventeen seconds—calibrated against previous non-bearded notations—per airport."

"I don't believe you, Ravi," I said. "You must have done a Mr. Bean-draws-a-gun or scowled at them to attract attention."

"But, of course, yaar, I had to make them notice my beard; I was not blessed with Karim Bhai's hairy effulgence. And anyway, some experiments need a catalyst."

A GLASS FULL OF LOVE

It was one of those Sundays when all three of us were home. When relaxing in the flat, Karim went about in a long embroidered kurta and white pajamas (stiffly ironed): he sat there in this home wear, the door of his room wide open, trying to surf news channels on an old desktop that stood (covered with plastic when not in use) in a corner of his room. Ravi wore his casually expensive shorts and emblazoned T-shirt, and I was fully dressed, in jeans and a shirt: Ravi had once noted that this was what proved my professional middle-class status, that only members of the upper classes and the lower or lower middle-classes in the subcontinent wore casual or Indian clothes in company.

Karim came out of his room. He looked disgusted.

"I should buy a new computer. This one is so slow," he said to us. We were in the kitchen, watching BBC on a small TV that Karim had installed atop the fridge. He had a slightly bigger plasma TV on a wall of his room.

"Why don't you, Karim Bhai? They are quite cheap now and you must be minting millions with all the extra shifts you do," Ravi replied lightly.

Karim Bhai took the suggestion seriously. He did not always get light banter.

"Oh, I am not making that much money, you know," he said. "And I have expenses..."

He always claimed he had "expenses" but never elaborated on the nature of these.

"You can use my laptop, Karim Bhai." Mine was plugged in on the kitchen table and it was much faster than Karim's antique machine. We were used to such situations by now: Karim would get fed up with his slow desktop, one of us would offer him one of our faster laptops, he would refuse, as was proper; the offer would have to be repeated; he would accept with formal thanks, and spend about an hour surfing for news, mostly from India and various Muslim nations.

Those days with Tunisia, Egypt, Libya, all on the boil, he was particularly interested in the news. So were we—it was one of the sources of Ravi's frustration with Danish universities that our students seemed unaware of what was happening. But there was an obvious difference in our interest in the events of what I preferred to call the Jasmine Revolution and Ravi, with greater skepticism, termed the Twitter Twister. Ravi and I had opinions; we were members of democratic chat groups, we signed Avaaz petitions, our Facebooks were cluttered with radical quotations. But Karim Bhai simply went to the news pages, in English, Urdu and Arabic, read them so closely that his beard touched the keyboard; he never commented on anything. If he said something, it was usually very general: "It is better today," or "It is a bit worse, I think."

"It is better today in Cairo," he said, after browsing for half an hour. He brought out his pouch and started rolling himself a cigarette.

By then Ravi had taken a shower and was dressed in a selection of his best jeans, shirt and pullover. It meant he was going out to see a woman. Ravi refused to go for walks on Sundays, claiming that a Sunday walk in the woods or the parks was a deeply religious act in Denmark. His argument ran like this: Protestants had started substituting God with Nature a long time back; there is nothing more religious than a Protestant going for a walk on a Sunday; it is the Protestant version of Sunday church-going. If Ravi had to do something religious, he said, he would do it consciously and openly; he would (and sometimes did) go to church on Sundays.

As Ravi had resolutely refused to say anything about Lena after returning from London, I was curious about his sartorial efforts that Sunday, more so because he had totally stopped going out with or being visited by any of his "plain" girlfriends. But I knew better than to quiz Ravi. Despite his seeming loquacity, he could be very tight-lipped on some matters.

"You seem to follow Cairo a lot, Karim Bhai," I responded.

"I was there, you know. Didn't I tell you?"

"Lucky you, Karim Bhai. I wish I could go there for a long vacation," shouted Ravi from his room. The trace of some expensive aftershave wafted from his room. Ravi had been planning to go to Cairo for years.

"No, Ravi Bhai," Karim corrected him, "I wasn't there as a tourist. I studied there. I did my BA in Islamic jurisprudence and Arabic from Cairo."

Ravi entered the kitchen, shirt still unbuttoned. He was intrigued.

"Cairo, Karim Bhai?" he asked. "I did not know Indian students went to Egypt to study."

"Some do. There are a few scholarships, mostly for poor Muslim students," Karim explained apologetically.

Ravi looked enlightened. He turned to me and said, almost forgetting that Karim was in the room: "See, bastard, and people like us only know of scholarships to the West! Wish I had known: I could have converted and gone to Cairo!"

"It is not that different from Delhi," said Karim Bhai dismissively. "But, you see, I have friends there, so I get a bit worried..."

"Girlfriends too, I daresay, Karim Bhai," Ravi teased him, as he sometimes did.

Karim Bhai blushed.

"Oh no," he said, "we got married." I almost spilled my coffee.

"I did not know you were married, Karim Bhai," Ravi blurted in surprise.

"Oh, didn't I mention it before? It was such a long time back. Thirty years ago, almost..."

"And, Karim Bhai..."

"Yes," Karim Bhai interrupted, ruminating, "twenty-six years ago..."

"But Karim Bhai," Ravi could not restrain himself, the aunties in him were clamoring for gossip. "What happened? We have never even seen a photo of..."

"I do not take or keep photos, Ravi Bhai. You know that it is against my religion," Karim explained. And it was true, though I doubt that either Ravi or I had noticed it before: the flat was shorn of even a single representation of a human being, animal or bird. Karim did not even seem to have a photo album in his room.

Karim Bhai was talking again: "What happened, Ravi Bhai? Who knows?" He looked at me, and at that moment we thought we understood what might have happened. "Who knows what happens to us in this world and why?" he continued ruefully.

"Only Allah-tala knows." Then he quoted from the Quran: "Allah has knowledge of all things."

I had once said to Ravi: if you dislike this place so much, why did you apply for a PhD here?

"I applied to Stockholm, Copenhagen and Oslo too," he had replied. "They gave me a full scholarship here."

"But why Scandinavia, Ravi?"

"What choice did I have, bastard? Every Tom, Dick and Hari from India goes to USA, UK, Australia or Canada for a PhD these days. Look at what it does to them! Look at yourself, yaar. And I thought, well, I had enough German, might as well pick up another language through it and see what happens to civilization when it freezes."

I am certain Ravi was not joking when he exclaimed that he would have converted and gone to Egypt.

I recall that Sunday for two other unusual happenings. Both of them involved women and Karim Bhai, which was unusual in itself. Isn't that one of the twists of life? You spend weeks in the flat of a man who seems to have no relations with women, who does not even allow himself to sit alone in a room with a woman, and the day he reveals that he had once been married is also the day when he has intimate meetings with two other women? Oh, I am exaggerating: the intimacy was only of the emotional sort.

But there is no doubt that, whatever the causes, both women came to Karim Bhai in an obviously emotional state.

Ravi disappeared on his bicycle soon after our Cairo conversation, hunting out both his cycle lamps and his cycle clips, which indicated his intention to stay out until night and his desire to reach his destination in a high state of sartorial elegance. He wore his favorite leather jacket and his patent gloves too. I think I was still digesting the notion of Karim Bhai once being married when the doorbell rang.

Ajsa walked in with her Somali husband, Ibrahim, and Ali, who, I had been told, was inseparable from Ibrahim. They offered only a perfunctory nod to me—my door was open and I was revising a lecture at my small study table—and walked into Karim Bhai's room. Karim Bhai closed the door of his room behind them. This was unusual, as you know; he seldom closed his door completely. But I did not mind. I had never liked Ali, with his saliva-spraying religious virulence, and I had never met Ibrahim. In fact, I still think this was the only time I saw him: such a fleeting glimpse that when I came across his photo in the papers much later, I did not recognize the man.

For the next hour or so, I heard their voices rise and hush in argument: the high tones came from Ali and, once or twice, Ajsa. They were speaking Danish—the only language all of them really shared—and all I could gather was that they were talking about Islam and insults to Islam at least once in a while. Of course, I might have imagined this later on; at that moment, annotating my lecture on *Gulliver's Travels*, I did not really pay them too much attention.

Perhaps I really noticed that they had been arguing when Ali stalked out and, banging both the doors shut, left the flat.

Ibrahim followed him less than a minute later, leaving the door to Karim Bhai's room ajar. But this, of course, was not sufficient for Karim Bhai. I heard him come to my door. He scratch-knocked on it and then put his head in, beard first. "Would you like to join Ajsa and me for a cup of tea?" he asked.

I had almost finished revising my lecture and, in any case, I was curious about the argument. I joined Karim and Ajsa in his room. She was sitting on the sofa. It looked like she had been crying. There were two plastic folding chairs—Karim Bhai kept six piled in a corner for his Quran sessions—next to the sofa. I took one of them. Karim Bhai bustled around, brewing tea. He was in such a rush or so agitated that he brewed it the Danish way and brought it in on a tray, with a pot of sugar and a carton of cold milk from the fridge.

Ajsa did not say much. Mostly they talked of the weather. When she got up to leave, Karim did something unusual. He put a hand on her shoulder. I wondered how many brownie points this gesture cost him in his paradise. She was a bit taller than him, so he had to look up at her. "Don't worry," he told her, squeezing her shoulder gingerly, "I will take care of it. I will talk to Ibrahim soon."

The second female visitor Karim received that Sunday was just as unexpected. She had been there before, of course, but never so abruptly, and in such mental disarray.

I had agreed to cook dinner. Karim Bhai ate around Danish time, and we had gotten used to it too. It was a bit after six in the evening.

My cooking is not as elaborate as Ravi's or as practiced, if limited, as Karim Bhai's. I usually slice onions, tomatoes and whatever else might be within slicing distance, fry it with chicken or minced meat or, in Denmark, salmon, add salt according to taste as they say, and finally plop in a bottle of Uncle Ben's jalfrezi or some such ready-made mix of spices. It goes with rice, seldom Basmati, or pasta.

I had just plunked in Uncle Ben's korma mix when the bell rang. Karim, who was puttering around tidying up the flat, both TVs showing the same Danish news, went to open the door. There were muttered exchanges in Danish. I assumed it was some neighbor or a Jehovah's Witness. But in a few seconds, Karim re-entered the kitchen with Pernille, Great Claus's wife from upstairs.

"Perhaps Pernille can eat with us," he said to me.

Pernille declined, but we insisted; she looked tired—the Eng Lit description, in Ravi-speak, would have been "haggard and woebegone"—and did not need much persuasion. Karim Bhai bustled about in the kitchen, relieving me of the chore of cooking the rice. Karim Bhai cooked only seven or eight dishes—halal restrictions curtailed his scope—but he cooked them well and always in a pressure cooker. I didn't, dreading its whistle and the hint of a coming explosion. The rice, thanks to the intervention of Karim and his pressure cooker, was ready much quicker than it would have been if I had cooked it.

After the table had been laid and the rice and curry placed in the middle, we plied Pernille with the fare. She pecked at the food, only perking up once to compliment the cooking. It was sheer politeness.

"Where is Claus Bhai?" asked Karim Bhai finally, perhaps just to break the awkward silence.

"I wish I knew," replied Pernille, with some asperity. "I thought he might be here. That's why I knocked..."

Claus did drop in regularly—the only Dane I ever met who did not require an appointment at least a week in advance—and sometimes he and Little Claus joined us for dinner or lunch. But we had not seen him that day.

"He must be working," suggested Karim Bhai.

"If only..." said Pernille. But then, with characteristic reserve, she changed the subject.

Later, after she had left, Karim Bhai looked at me and shook his head.

"Things are not going well between them," he said to me.

I was not sure: Pernille sounded like a woman who had unconsciously or consciously compromised on her career for the sake of her children, and the children had inevitably flown the coop.

"No, no," replied Karim Bhai, "I have known them for many many years. Things have not been good between them for a long time."

"Why, Karim Bhai?" I could not help asking.

Karim hesitated. I knew he avoided anything that resembled gossip. Then he said in a low monotone: "Pernille thinks that Claus is having, that Claus is... (He lowered his voice a bit further, so much that I had to crane forward to follow him)... seeing another, you know, another woman."

He blushed. It had cost him effort to mention the possibility. And he hastened to add: "But, of course, he is not. Claus is a decent man. It is just that, here, you know here... (He waved his short arms around to indicate all of Denmark and perhaps all of Europe)... here everyone has such suspicions, everyone is always afraid. I keep telling her that it is not true, and she keeps saying that she will never forgive Claus if, after all these years, he leaves her for another woman."

I did not see Ravi that night or the next morning. He must have slept over somewhere else. But he walked into my office on Monday afternoon and said, in lieu of a greeting: "I ran into some of your Eng Lit First World types in the psycho canteen. I think I will avoid the place in the future: it is infested by Eng Lit types."

"Why, what did they do to you?" I asked, not really interested. I knew it was just a prelude to banter for Ravi.

"Do? Eng Lit First World types never do anything. That is why they are Eng Lit First World types. You see, bastard, I was having this gloriously political conversation with some guys from the French and Spanish departments, when in walk a group of Eng Lit types. They know some of us, so they join us; I continue lambasting Mubarak and the Egyptian army and the Twitter Twister. Then in steps one of your Eng Lit types with his two cents of political observation and quotes Yeats. Can you guess what he quotes?"

"No."

"Oh, c'mon, yaar, give it a try. It is what you Eng Lit types quote habitually when you need to talk pol-eee-ticks. I have had it quoted at me at least fifteen times, and always by Eng Lit types. I'll give you a hint: 'passionate intensity.'"

"The best lack all conviction, the worst are full of passionate intensity."

"Bullseye, O Eng Lit type!" exclaimed Ravi in his best theatrical mode.

"How nightmarish," I rejoined mockingly.

"That's an understatement. I observed that, personally, I prefer even shorter poems. I quoted Campbell: 'You praise the firm restraint with which they write./ I am there with you, of course:/ They use the snaffle and the curb all right,/ But where's the bloody horse.' You know what he said?"

"That it is a minor poem?"

"Exactly. Your perception is to be maha-commended, Eng Lit type. It proves that you are Eng Lit (Third World Category) type, so that while you too waste your life worrying about the exact shades of the two-tone shoes worn by Billy Great Shakes, you manage to notice, unlike your First World colleagues, the mud and horse shit on Shakespeare's shoes too. You are right; your colleague, or whoever it was, looked surprised. But it is a minor poem, he said mincingly. I looked him in the eye and pronounced: it is not the missing poem that concerns me; it is the fucking missing horse."

Then he added, as if it was an afterthought, though I realized that this was what he had come to my office to say: "Reminds me: don't you think it is time you met Lena?"

It was then I was certain that this was different. Ravi had never offered to introduce me to any of his girlfriends in the past and that too with such brusque tentativeness.

Ravi later told me that he had finally confessed to Lena how he felt about her two days after he returned from his trip to London and Amsterdam. That trip was not just the culmination of his beard experiment; it was also his attempt to avoid making that confession to Lena. He had tried to push her away. He thought he had succeeded. But the day after he returned, he met her for coffee—knowing Ravi, it was probably a conscious testing of his will—and, as he put it, he "fell in love with her all over again, yaar."

The very next day he had asked her to join him for lunch at the Milano pizzeria. I was surprised. Milano pizzeria was a tacky place frequented only by students.

"You mean you confessed your blooming love to her under the plaster statue of that woman, what is it, Athena-taking-to-purdah or spider-woman-entangled-in-her-own-web, hanging from the wall?" I mocked.

"The very place, bastard. But not under that statue. I said it next to the smaller one of Laurel and Hardy, by the window." He laughed.

This is how it seems to have happened. I am putting it together now, from the various bits and pieces that Ravi revealed, sometimes unintentionally, over the next few weeks.

They had ordered the usual lunch pizza, which you get for thirty crowns, a free Coke or Fanta thrown in. Lena, being vegetarian, had gone for a margherita. Ravi, as he almost always did, had ordered a pepperoni. Lena took a Coke; Ravi a Fanta.

When I try to imagine the occasion, in my mind Milano pizzeria is not crowded. There are only four students at a far table. Not that Lena or Ravi would have noticed, I suspect. Outside, a bit of sunshine falls on the parked cars. Inside, the large TV screen up on the wall shows an MTV song, all gyrating hips and jerking boobs, being safely "radical" in the only way permitted in the West these days. Ravi and Lena do not watch the flashing images, their cascade of empty signs. They have eyes only for each other.

"She looked at me with those green eyes, and I knew what I had to say. The words might sound corny to you, bastard, but at that moment, they were the only words I could have uttered."

Ravi's glass of Fanta was half-full. He looked at it.

He said to Lena, "You know, one goes through life and is grateful for the love one gets and gives. It is never exactly what one has dreamed of or what one is capable of. The glass is never more than half-full. But even that is a gift; so many people do not get even that. I have been lucky in my relationships; I have had my glasses filled to half again and again, and sometimes perhaps even a bit more. I have never expected anything more."

I imagine Ravi smiling ironically and philosophically here. Lena was looking intently into his eyes. There was an expression of surprise on her face, almost. Ravi had continued: "But when I saw you at Unibar that night, I realized for the first time that, at least for me, the glass can be full. That it can brim over. It was frightening, this knowledge. I tried to push it away. But I could not. I know now that I do not care what you feel; I am grateful to discover that, yes, our glasses can fill to the brim. That it is possible. Just that knowledge is enough, and I wanted to thank you for it."

What had Lena said to him in reply? He didn't tell me then. He simply told me that they were together now and that he wanted me to meet her. We agreed to meet at a seminar reception that evening, which he would be attending with Lena. But later on, I think he told me what she had said on that occasion. This was many weeks later, when matters had taken a difficult turn for all of us, and not just because of Karim Bhai.

I remember Ravi telling me then, weeks later, in a reminiscent mood, "Do you know, yaar, what Lena said when I confessed my feelings to her? She told me that she had never felt this way about a man before, that the moment she walked into Unibar, she knew she had a crush on me, that cycling back later that night, she almost hit the curb a few times because all she could think of was... you know... me."

But by then Ravi, with his usual inability to leave matters unexamined, had started picking at vestiges of his own memory of the moment and peeling away, layer by layer, the meanings, intended or not, of a casual word like "crush." I will have to come to that part of my story too, but in between there lies a glorious summer of love.

It was the usual kind of post-seminar reception. The bare university room, with wide windows on one side, had been arranged with tables and chairs, wooden, utilitarian, minimalist, with subdued colors, the kind of furniture that I now instantly associate with Scandinavia. The tables bore large and light aluminum trays holding open sandwiches: there were bowls of chips and bottles of soft drinks and wine. There were plastic cups and paper plates.

Ravi was late. When he walked in with Lena, I was struck by what a striking pair they made. Of course, they did not walk in as a couple; in the eyes of the assemblage, they were just PhD students coming to a reception together. But a couple is what they were: the broader beauty of Ravi's Bollywood looks somehow matching the narrow perfection of Lena's Nordic features; his jet-black hair set off by her cascading dark golden locks; his light-brown eyes complementing her surprisingly green ones. They did not stay together for long, as both of them knew different people in the room, and both of them came from classes where one circulates democratically.

But even when they were at opposite ends of the room, there seemed a current between them. I recognized it: there was a time when my ex and I, in the earliest weeks of our relationship, had felt something similar, much weaker but similar, about each other. This was before time had interfered, with its slow erosion of the cliffs of certainty, its full storms and hollow caves. But never had I shared

63

something exactly like this with my ex or any woman I had been in love with. I would have been envious if I did not love Ravi like the brother I never had.

Ravi and Lena moved in tandem, even when they were in different groups. They had ears for each other while they were holding a conversation—easy, attentive, graceful—with other people. Even their backs had eyes for each other.

They were both highly polished in their social skills: people who were born naturally elegant and had honed their elegance to perfection. Ravi, in his own couldn't-care-less way, with his clothes just a bit but stylishly awry, his long hair ruffled and loosely curling; Lena in her closely coiffured and dressed, highly reserved manner, everything always in place.

I remember thinking: they will probably stay elegant, in different ways; Ravi with quicksilver ebullience, effusively, Lena with icy calm, on the deck of any sinking Titanic.

They circulated and conversed with ease, plastic glasses of wine poised, sparkling. With my prior knowledge, it was difficult to understand how the company around us failed to see what I saw. Even though Lena and Ravi were excellent conversationalists, with a dozen languages between them, it was obvious to me that their conversation assumed a special sparkle only when they were in the same circle.

For me, though, infected surely by Ravi's enthusiasm and sense of wonderment at what had happened between them, it was like a miracle gone unremarked: as if someone was walking on water while people went about their barbecue parties all over the beach, poking sausage and salting steak on their grills, and guzzling down beer.

THE SUN ALSO RISES

Ravi snuggled comfortably into the Native American blanket that he often used for a shawl indoors.

"You see, bastard," he said, "you as a bloody Mussalman from the Land of the fucking Pure have only two options in the lands of Unbelievers if you want to intrigue a damsel in distrust. Either you talk about how you, at the age of fourteen, broke into your piggy bank and stole money from your traditional dad's wallet to go whoring, or you talk about how you grew up praying five and a half times a day and admiring the mujahideen until, O Heart, O Torn and Riven Heart, as recently as a year ago you began to lose your faith—but, alas, not your confusion or anger. Give 'em either of the two narratives, and they'll beat yuh to the draw when it comes to dropping yer respective panties. But lookit yerself! Look at yourself, you sad unpackaged commodity! You talk about your schooling, which is like their schooling; you talk about your parents, who are like their parents; you talk about your life, which is like their life. They look at you and expect something else. You look like you are something else. And then you go ahead and disappoint them. And you, a fucking scholar of literature who should know better! Shame on you!"

"What about you, Ravi? How come you have been getting away with having more of their lives than they do themselves?"

"Not any more, bastard: I am a one-woman man now. It's only Lena for me. Never thought I would be like that, damn it, but I have no desire even to look at another woman."

"Still," I insisted, "let's consider your checkered career until you saw the, ahem, golden light."

"Ah well, it is different with me, Ignorant Human," he replied, sipping his coffee. "You see, I'm not just a wyrd buggah; I am a Hindoo from Inja. I can dance to the tune of a hundred instruments on the thousand arms of my million gods, half of them hermaphrodite. Moreover, thanks to you fundamentalist bastards, I am Prester John these days."

"Prester John?"

"Don't tell me you ain't never heard of Emperor Prester John, you half-injun?"

I had come across the name in books, but could not recall the connection.

Ravi continued in his oratorical mode, which had increased in scope and vibrancy ever since he dropped all his "plain" girlfriends for Lena: "You have missed something. See, this is the twelfth century, if I remember correctly. Ok? Twelfth century. Europeans are frightened of the Saracens. Suddenly, good news: it appears that on the other side of the Islamic threat there is a powerful Christian emperor, Prester John, just waiting to join forces with European crusaders. Hallelujah! For centuries, he is there, on the other side of every Islamic threat, real or imagined, about to come to the rescue of Christendom. Only, poor Prester John never existed."

"So?" I did not get the connection.

"So, over the centuries, a large number of Europeans have needed this mythical Prester John. Sometimes, when they get really desperate, they even Prester John a Muslim people, as they did with the Arabs when Lawrence of Arabia was waging his jihad against the Ottomans. Lately, behold, O Fanatical Believer, ancient Hindoo Inja is the new Prester John: the great non-Muslim ally on the other side of the crescent! We are in, old boy; they actually smile at Indian passports at Customs sometimes. The first time it happened to me, a few months after 9/11, I almost fainted with the shock. Our chances to lay la lasses increased triple-fold after 9/11. Provided we do not tie a turban around our heads, as some silly Sikhs still do, and get them all confused because they have seen cartoons depicting your Mohammad in a turban."

The history lesson about Prester John that Ravi had poured into my ears emanated mostly from his desire to fix me up with a girlfriend. He had always wanted to do that, ever since I got divorced. Most of it was concern for me—he suspected that I still missed my ex-wife. He was probably right: my divorce had been a difficult decision. I had still been partly in love with my wife, but I could no longer ignore the fact that, while she wanted children immediately, I had no desire to become a father.

The fact that we had tried naturally for a couple of years had been easy for me to overlook. But when she started insisting on us going to the clinic—there was nothing "wrong" with either of us, as the doctors told us, but she did not want to wait any longer—it made me face up to my own reluctance. I could no longer ignore it. Neither could I ignore my deep dislike of the clinic: it seemed to me, and still does, that we were forcing nature, when nature actually had not given us any real ground to use force against it. My wife had disagreed.

That morning with the plastic container and the patrol car had made up my mind, but my wife had not been able to accept the decision. I did not blame her: after all, it is the woman who bears a child, carries it around for nine months, suffers changes in her own body. And when we finally got divorced, I was saddened. My wife too, I am sure, but she felt that my refusal to return to the clinic was an indication of my lack of love for her. I wasn't convinced of that; she was. It made it easier for her to leave.

Ravi knew all this; Ravi and I seldom had secrets from each other—or, given the aunts in Ravi, at least I didn't have secrets from him. He must have felt that I needed a girlfriend. The sporadic dating I did was not enough, as he told me, and he never understood why I was so careful about entering another relationship.

"What are you waiting for, you Paki?" he asked me. "A houri from fucking paradise?"

I thought that his concern about my love life would diminish after he had hooked up with Lena. But now that he had himself found someone whom he obviously saw as a "houri from fucking paradise," he grew even more concerned. He wanted to fix me with a partner. There was always a romantic in Ravi, buried under a few tons of skepticism and irony: I am sure he liked to imagine us together, as paired couples, going for trips and walks and treks in the glorious Danish summer that was now around the corner.

"I don't believe in houris or paradise," I replied.

"Well," he mused, "don't be so bloody sure of it: I thought so too until I met Lena. But anyway, what's wrong? Why is it you have not found any pretty pige, merry mademoiselle or fine fräulein yet? What is so fucking wrong with all these lovely young ladies you have dated and dropped?"

"Nothing, Ravi. They were all lovely young ladies. They were just not my type."

"You mean there is no one in this fucking country who has ever moved your fancy? You know you are one picky Paki, pardner!"

"You know that's not what I mean."

"What is it that you mean, then?"

"Have I told you this joke about the man who was looking for a perfect girlfriend?"

"Don't switch the topic, bastard!"

"Listen. Ok? There is this man. He never dates a girl more than once. He goes on a date and never calls up that girl again. His doting mother is worried. She wants to be upgraded to granny. Go on, son, she urges him, find me a daughter-in-law soon. I will, I will, mom, the son replies, I am just waiting for my perfect woman. One evening he returns from a date and announces that he has found his perfect woman and that, actually, he is going to see her again the next night. Hallelujah, exclaims the mom. The next night she lights candles and stays up. The son is back early, looking morose. What's wrong, son, says mummy, seeing her promotion to granny receding, I thought you had found your perfect woman. I did, mom, replies the son, but you see, she is looking for her perfect man."

"So, who is this perfect woman of yours who rejected you, you poor Paki?"

"No perfect woman, Ravi; like houries, they do not exist... but of course, one meets women one likes who are obviously not interested."

"Nah!" he replied, shaking his head. "There are ways out of such dilemmas, mostly."

"For you, perhaps..."

"For everyone. Now you name me one woman you like, even vaguely, and who you think is not interested."

I named one of his colleagues in the history department, a recently divorced mother of one.

"Ms. Linen Marx!" exclaimed Ravi. "Never dreamed you fancied Miss Linen Marx!"

Ravi always called her Miss Linen Marx because she wore only cotton and linen garments and was, according to Ravi, the only Danish academic under fifty who had actually read Karl Marx.

He mulled over my revelation.

"I see," he hummed and hawed, "I see... Yes, bastard, that might be a hard nut to crack."

There, I retorted.

"For you, bastard. Because you see, O Eng Lit Type, thou typically dost not usest thine imagination..."

But he let the matter rest after that. Or so I thought.

Great Claus had not forgotten his promise to thank us with a "pucca mughlai dinner" for the night he had spent in Ravi's room. That month, he finally found a weekend evening—I think it was a Sunday—when Karim was not working and Ravi and I were free.

It was uncommon to find Ravi free in the evenings now. He was usually with Lena. Sometimes, when they went out in a group, I would join them. But, by and large, our evenings out were getting to be rare. Not that I minded: he was so obviously in love; both of them were. And I was trying to complete an academic study: a book on the impact of English Romanticism on Urdu literature in the nineteenth century. With tenure not in sight, I knew that I would have to start applying for jobs soon—and I needed a second scholarly book to stand a chance anywhere outside Denmark.

But that Sunday evening, all three of us were free and, as arranged, we knocked on Claus and Pernille's door at six o'clock sharp. We were carrying a bouquet and a box of chocolates between us. As Karim was going to be there, we could obviously not have brought a bottle or two of wine. Claus insisted on cooking halal and not serving alcohol in the presence of Karim: it was not the first time Claus and Pernille had hosted a dinner for him. I am certain Karim would not have eaten with people who took such matters lightly.

We had been to Claus and Pernille's flat before, but only for a drink or a coffee. This was the first time we were able to lounge around and look at the flat. It was a tastefully furnished place, with sleek metal and glass furniture and a large shiny kitchen that drew sincere praise even from Ravi. There were batik hangings on the walls and expensive reproductions of paintings. Even I could identify one of the limited-edition reproductions—the large-skulled and bloat-bellied man in a watery setting was unmistakable—as a painting by Michael Kvium. Ravi, who knew more about Danish art than I did, located other names—including an original canvas by Martin Bigum, whom I had not heard of.

Pernille and Claus had the kind of flat one associates with younger yuppie types, singles or willfully childless couples: immaculate, full of modern shiny furniture and expensive art objects. It seemed discrepant: they were people who had reared two children and, in their dress and appearance, looked like typical parents in their fifties. It was not the first time I wondered at the difference between what we seem to be and what we are to ourselves. Or is this too something that I think of now, penning down this account with all the advantages of hindsight?

Though Claus made an effort to be hearty (and he had cooked up a tropical storm of north Indian dishes from a cookbook by Madhur Jaffrey), the dinner was less than cheerful. Their twin daughters made an appearance, but just at the dining table. They had always struck me as among those surprising kids that Danish families produce: the ones who do not seem to feel any need to rebel against their parents or their values. Denmark, Ravi and I agreed on this, is particularly good at this—and though Ravi considered it a frighteningly conservative aspect of the country, I was not so sure. It is rare today to find parents and children sharing a space not riven with tensions and silences. Surely there must be something to admire in that.

But the dinner was shot through with tension. Much of it was aimed at Claus. The daughters hardly spoke to him over the table, and Pernille's remarks to him were sometimes laced with acid. Claus's usual repertoire of jokes—always well-meaning but seldom hilarious—fractured on the stone of his family's refusal to be humored and Karim's lack of interest in punch lines.

"Why doesn't the West eat with its fingers?" asked Claus, serving the Mughlai Murgh. He answered the question in the next breath: "Because its hands are not clean." His daughters and wife did not even look up from their plates; Karim managed a feeble smile only in order to emulate our effort.

Even Ravi, with the elegant magnanimity that enabled him to turn other people's embarrassment into jokes aimed at himself, could not always save the situation. We left early.

Going down the stairs, Karim Bhai, who knew more about our neighbors than he appeared to, commented on the matter.

"I don't understand Claus," he remarked, "I do not understand why he is behaving like this."

I was surprised. It had appeared to me that poor Claus had been at the receiving end all evening, and that he had treated his family with much consideration despite the provocations. Karim Bhai obviously knew more, but he was not the type of person who would gossip. And Ravi, who might have drawn the information out of him on some earlier occasion, was too happily lost in Lena now to have much time for the inquisitive aunts in himself.

We still had a lot to discover, and not least about Karim Bhai.

Why does this memory come back to me, almost entirely, exactly in this part of my attempt to recollect and understand what really happened to all of us?

I think I have already said that I almost never attended Karim

Bhai's Quran sessions on Fridays. But sometimes I waited for Ravi to finish with them, and once or twice—when we had appointments elsewhere—even went in to fetch him. This must have been one of those times. I am not absolutely certain, but I remember Karim Bhai—he always sat in the left corner of his sagging sofa—and a crowd of serious young faces around him. And I can, at this moment, distinctly recall what he was saying, as I waited for Ravi to get up and leave with me.

"The Prophet, peace be upon him," said Karim Bhai, with that irritating glaze in his dark-edged eyes that fellow-Muslims often get when speaking of the founder of the religion, "had only one wife for years: she was about twenty years older than him. He remained faithful to her and he did not marry again until after she died, peace be upon her. In fact, for a long time, she was among the very few who believed in his message. You can say that she believed in the message of Allah before the Holy Prophet did himself, for when the Holy Prophet heard the message for the first time, he thought he was hearing voices. She was the person who convinced him that it was a genuine revelation."

"Women have a lot to answer for," I whispered to Ravi in the lobby, who frowned and hushed me. No matter how flippant Ravi was about matters that concerned me, including the religion I was born into, he was always a very polite listener in the case of Karim Bhai.

Karim Bhai was just as polite while listening to Ravi. With me, he showed some signs of impatience, subdued, betrayed only by the eyes flicking to the TV screen or the hands picking up a newspaper while I was talking critically about matters like the Islamization of Pakistan. But with Ravi, Karim would make an effort, focus on his words with his possibly kohled eyes, his forehead wrinkling sometimes in a bid to follow Ravi's somersaulting conversation.

What was he listening for in Ravi's case? Those barbs about Western hubris that, though they came from a different source, soothed the Islamist in Karim? Or was he interested in Ravi as a person who could be converted to Karim's cause, whatever that was? Or, and this polar opposite was possible too, was he observing Ravi as one would observe an alien from outer space?

Or was it something simpler: Karim's respect for someone who was from another culture, or class?

In any case, Karim would listen carefully to Ravi's conversation, and Ravi, in his turn, would offer his opinions in uncharacteristically modulated and less acerbic terms. For instance, he would not dismiss the existence of God but simply mention the fact that it did not mesh with the evidence of human suffering. At which Karim would shake his head and gently disagree, trotting out all the arguments that the believing have used for centuries to avoid being faced with their loneliness in the universe.

The debate would continue, gently, in the kitchen. I would retire to my room to read or take a nap. I did not really know who was trying to convert whom, and I did not care. I had given up on God a long time back; if God had existed, I am sure he would have reciprocated in kind.

We were on our way to a party thrown by one of Ravi's PhD colleagues. I knew the person only vaguely, but he had invited me and Ravi had insisted on me coming along: his argument was that he would feel more comfortable going there with Lena and me, than with Lena alone. Both of them were remarkably careful about their relationship in public: revealing it fully only in contexts where, they felt, it would not be devalued into something else, something more mundane, something like the usual academic affair between two attractive PhD students.

We met Lena for a drink in a café in town, before heading for the party. She was wearing a one-shoulder turquoise chiffon evening dress that brought out her intensely green eyes, her golden hair tied into one of those intricate knots that are again coming back into vogue. When I had seen them together the first time, I had been struck by how similar they were despite their differences. This time, I was struck by how different they were despite their similarities. Ravi was consciously unguarded, in behavior, opinion and dress; his speech was full of gaps and curlicues; his shirt was never too ironed, his hair always a bit awry. Lena was controlled and guarded: every bit of dress and hair in place, every word and gesture so carefully enunciated or performed that she seemed to be on stage all the time. It needed someone with Ravi's casual and unassuming confidence to fall in love with her, as he claimed to have fallen in love: the full glass and not the usual half glasses that we usually subsist on. Many other men would have found her frightening and cold, for Lena was a woman who had either become her own mask or never let that mask down in public. Perhaps, I thought, she did for Ravi. Perhaps that was what knitted them together, for at that point there was no doubt in my mind that this was not just a casual spring fling for either of them.

After Ravi had stopped to buy a good bottle of wine and some Belgian beers—he never trusted the alcohol served in Danish parties—we headed for his colleague's flat. It was a one-bedroom affair, with a large sitting-room-cum-kitchen. The kitchen had been arranged to resemble a bar from one side, with a half wall that had bar stools ranged against it. It was the kind of flat one would expect a bachelor to have.

And it was already crowded. Many of Ravi's colleagues were there and another dozen people or so, half of whom I knew or recognized from the university. All the chairs, stools and sofas were occupied; some people were ensconced on the bed in the bedroom.

The kitchen tables were lined with bottles, glasses and bowls of chips; two pizzas were in the oven and the chili con carne and rice almost ready. There wasn't going to be anything fancier: the decades when parties thrown by bachelors had to be redeemed from the shadow of Oedipal heterosexuality by offerings of a dozen intricate cuisines were over. Blokishness reigned in Denmark and heterosexual men were again free to be, in Ravi-speak, the uncouth pigs they naturally were.

But this blokishness did not encompass a carte blanche to smoke in the flat: Cancer was bigger than either Mars or Venus. There was a balcony attached to the bedroom. It was small and could contain only four or five people, standing, at a time. That was where smokers had to go to light up. It was seldom crowded, though: most of the people in the party were professional academics in their thirties and forties and their habits, like their books, accorded with the times.

Ravi headed for the balcony after a quick round of hellos, as he was offered a "bong" by someone he knew who spoke with an Australian accent. Bong, I assumed, was a kind of hash, something Ravi indulged in at parties. Lena fell in with people she knew, listening with the sort of expression of delighted interest that she brought into any conversation and that, undoubtedly, made many men feel more intelligent than they were. It was a talent she was not even fully aware of. Perhaps she saw it as courtesy or kindness.

An hour later, when the rice and the chili con carne had been ladled out and I was trying my best to balance my plate on my knees, sip from my glass, which was jostling for space with seven other glasses of different shapes on a small side table, and converse with migrating acquaintances, Ravi wended his way out of the bedroom, dodging a dozen pair of hands busy expressing ideas or conveying food.

"There he is," he said on catching sight of me, "I told you he is around…"

Behind him there walked a woman in her thirties, almost straw-blonde (though I later discovered that she dyed her hair), a bit short by Danish standards, but with the kind of rounded hips and slightly fleshy calves that I always notice. I knew her. This was the woman I had mentioned to Ravi, the one he called (behind her back, I am sure) Ms. Linen Marx.

I knew why Ravi had dragged her to my section of the party. I had more trouble understanding why Ms. Marx—let us call her that, for there are reasons (which will be revealed in due linear course, as my MFA-girlfriend would have insisted) to keep her name under cover—had allowed Ravi to drag her to me. She had not only shown no interest in me in the past, she had actually conveyed active disinterest on the one occasion when I had tried to break the ice. It had been done politely; it had struck me as genuine disinterest. She had not been bad to me: I was just not the kind of man she found interesting. How had Ravi managed to drag her through this crowd of coagulating con carne and conversations to my corner? I could only attribute it to the fact that women in general, married or not, interested or not, could seldom resist following Ravi around.

Not only did Ms. Marx follow Ravi to my corner, she showed no inclination to leave even after Ravi spotted Lena and abandoned us for her, with (or did I imagine it?) an almost imperceptible wink at me. I offered my seat to Ms. Marx. This woke some ghost of a non-blokish past in the man sitting next to me and he made a bit of space. Ms. Marx, to my surprise, wriggled in between the two of us, her wine glass held at a careful length in rounded bare arms (she was wearing a sleeveless dress of the sort that left most of the back bare too) which I tried not to look at. The blokes around me were not aware of either her arms, which rippled with the soft muscles of regular gym workouts, or her back. That, I have always felt, is the problem with being a bloke. It makes you ignore or vulgarize some of the best things in life.

I wondered whether Ravi considered Ms. Marx plain. I thought that she probably fell within the range of that demarcation for him, though in its higher reaches. It was a definition I would never have applied to Ms. Marx, even though I would not attain the glass-spilling exuberance of Ravi's love for Lena either. In any case, Ms. Marx—unlike Lena—was not the kind of woman who caught any man's eye; just as, to be honest, I am by no means the kind of man who turns every woman's head, at least for a second, as Ravi does. I believe people like Ms. Marx and me receive only half glasses of love and admiration and, at least in my case, that is sufficient.

I was not sure if it was sufficient in Ms. Marx's case, though. I knew she was divorced, with a child she shared with her ex (with whom she was, as is said, "very good friends"), and I have always suspected that divorced parents who stay good friends tend to have separated not because of any incompatibility but because they yearned for more than half-filled glasses in their lives.

Not only did Ms. Marx join me, she spent most of the party with me. Towards midnight, when the beer momentarily washes away the inhibitions of Danes, she asked me if I wanted to go out for a walk. The moon was almost full and it was surprisingly clear. Providence had rigged things in my favor for a change.

We kissed, more formally than passionately, on our way back to the flat.

Had I been less interested in Ms. Marx, I suppose I would have suspected Ravi's hand in her sudden interest in me. Or perhaps not, for it is difficult to imagine how any man can get a woman interested in another man. In any case, I had little time or inclination for suspicion. I saw Ms. Marx twice that week. Her interest in me grew every day; she wanted to know everything about me. Sometimes, she asked the same question again, in a slightly modified form, as if she did not believe my first version or wanted to hear it all over again.

The next week, on our third date, I was invited into her row-house flat for a nightcap. Her son, she said, was out on a camping trip with his father for the weekend, exploring some Jutland heath. Consequently, we spent the night at her place, exploring each other.

Next morning, we had a lazy breakfast. I rustled up an omelette, Indian-style, which usually impresses European women used to omelettes that are either flaccid and tasteless or stuffed with too many things to go for breakfast. She asked me how my parents had met; I told her they had been colleagues in the same university. Different departments, but same university. She lifted an eyebrow in surprise.

"They met at a political demonstration at their university. It turned out that a cousin of my father's was a friend of my mother's brother. I think that made it easier for them to keep seeing each other. A year later they got their parents to arrange a wedding for them."

Ms. Marx laughed in disbelief. "Why are you making this up?" she said.

I assured her that I was not making it up.

She left her chair and came over to me. She put her arms around my neck and squeezed affectionately. Her hair fell over my eyes.

"Remember, I am a historian: I expect consistency in historical accounts," she said. She pulled my chair back from the table—Ms. Marx was pretty strong for her size—and sat in my lap, straddling me. She smelled of orange yogurt. I kissed her. She tasted of orange yogurt too. We ended up making love on the kitchen floor.

It was close to noon when I returned to Karim's flat. I planned to take a leisurely shower and relax for the rest of the day, savoring the moments of last night and that morning: the slow friction of our flesh, the instant when I entered her, her soft grainy moistness, the smell of her sex, her lips all over me, kissing, sucking, the unhurried rhythm of sex between people who are old enough to know what they are about. I wanted to lie in bed and recall her breasts, which were small and surprisingly girl-like, her arms, which were fleshy and slightly muscular, her hips, her hair, her legs... I was not madly in love with her, but I did not have to be madly, or even eccentrically, in love. Sane attraction was what I wanted. It was enough.

I knew Karim Bhai would be on a day shift and I expected Ravi to be gone: he seldom spent the weekend in the flat anymore. Early on Saturday morning, if they had not already met on Friday night, as soon as he returned from his morning jog, Ravi would grab a toast, slurp some coffee and pedal off to Lena's flat, armed with aftershave and bike clips.

But when I walked into the flat, Ravi was still there, writing on his laptop.

"Bastard," he shouted to me from the kitchen, when I was still in the lobby, "you kept me waiting!"

I asked him why he had waited for me. We did not have any plans for the weekend.

Ravi laughed. Then he said, hazarding a guess, "Actually, I was wondering what you are going to tell Ms. Marx about your dad now."

It was then that the suspicion dawned on me.

"What have you been telling her about my parents, bastard?" I asked him.

"Just, as they say in America, like, the truth, pal."

"Like the truth?"

"Well, we all know how it is with you fucking fundus in Pak: veiled mother, bearded father, married at the age of fifteen, son divided between his halal mentality and the desire to make it in the pork-eating West, unwilling to acknowledge his religious background in public and unable to relinquish it in private, etcetera, etcetera."

I was flabbergasted.

"You didn't tell her all that, Ravi!" I exclaimed.

"Not at once, of course. I did it over days, weeks. For the sake of our friendship, sentimental music! I sacrificed hours of pleasure with Lena. Ms. Marx was kind of primed by the time I sprung her on you at the party, bastard, but I still had to keep selling you... Bits and pieces you know, yaar. You are damned good at queering your own pitch. You were so bloody intent on committing sexual harakiri by making your parents sound like her parents; I had to administer narrative antidotes all the time. I think she is convinced that you make up stories about your parents because you are too embarrassed or afraid to acknowledge your incipient provincial fundamentalism in these, ah, cosmopolitan circles. It appeals to both the Linen and the Marx in her."

I was so shocked I think I had to sit down. Used though I was to Ravi's chutzpah, this was still unexpected. When I recovered, I looked him in the eye and said, "Dammit, bastard, you know I am going to explain all this to her at the first opportunity, and she will drop me."

"Don't be too sure of that, O Unimaginative Teacher of Eng Lit," he replied, unplugging his laptop, probably on his way to Lena's now. "You see, it works like this. You buy a product because it is packaged as bing. What you get is bang. But, mostly, you discover that you quite like bang. That is how capitalism works, bastard: it promises you bing and gives you bang. There is a chance, Sir Adjunkt, that Ms. Marx likes you for bang now. Violins! Play on, if music be the tandoori of love..." With that he left, whistling "Il n'a jamais, jamais connu de loi..."

Ravi was not entirely wrong. When I disclosed Ravi's prank to Ms. Marx—I put it in the light of a practical joke played by him and she never conceded that it might have influenced her to start dating me—a shadow of irritation crossed her face. Two small vertical creases appeared between her eyebrows; I now know that they are a sign of anger. But then she laughed. And she agreed to see me again.

For the first time in my years in Denmark, I heard the sounds of domestic strife as I walked up the stairs that night. The evidence I had seen all around me—even the statistics of a nearly 50 percent divorce rate, which, Ravi perversely claimed, was slightly less disturbing than the statistics of a one percent divorce rate in India. But I had never heard the sounds of domestic strife. Not in Denmark.

The sounds came from the twin-flat of Great Claus and Pernille. First, a torrent of high-pitched Danish words (which I did not understand) from Pernille. Then a great booming "nej, nej, nej, jeg har sagt nej"—no, no, no, I have said no—from Claus, which was rudimentary and loud enough for me to understand. Then china or glass being smashed on the floor, a language that needs no interpretation across cultures. The slamming of a door. And then that loudest of noises: silence.

THE PRINCIPAL CLAUS

Ravi had spent the 1st of May trying to find a single public event or protest in the city that was, in his words, worthy of the occasion. It was an annual ritual with him. As usual, he had failed.

But this year, he took the disappointment quite well. He did not talk about how Denmark was the only modern country that never had and never would have a revolution, or try to explain why this peculiar quirk of Danish history could be traced to the mid-nineteenth century founding of the Tivoli Entertainment Park, for the distraction of the people, in Copenhagen. He even ignored the usual rhetoric put forth by the usual Danish politicians calling for the abolishment of Labor Day and its replacement by the Queen's Birthday as a "truly Danish event."

I had noticed this in recent weeks: his love for Lena had made him less critical, or at least more forgiving. It made me overcome the irritation that I felt at times at Ravi's tolerance of Karim Bhai's more Islamic habits. Ravi, despite all his cracks, was someone who put people first. In those days, not uninfluenced by a lecture I had written on Swift, I saw in Ravi the shade of that caustic Irish writer who, in response to his critics, had claimed he did not hate humankind—because, unlike his critics, he was never surprised by human failings. Perhaps I was wrong in that too. Perhaps Ravi expected more from humankind than Swift. I am certain he expected more from Lena.

One morning, late in May, Karim Bhai turned to us over breakfast, with his dark-edged baby-eyes, and said, "Will both of you be here on Saturday afternoon next week? Ajsa wants to drop in and pick up her things."

Ajsa still had a few boxes and books stored away in the flat. It looked like she had finally found space for them in the place she shared with Ibrahim.

Ravi was going to be away for the weekend with Lena. He said so.

"Are you working on Saturday, Karim Bhai?" he asked.

"No, actually, I am not," replied Karim.

"Then you won't need us," said Ravi. "She just has some odds and ends. You will manage between the two of you."

Ravi, despite his interest in Karim's faith, could be surprisingly blind at times to its intensity and rigidity. I knew by now that Karim Bhai wanted one of us around because he would not allow himself to be alone in a flat with a woman he was not married to and who was not related to him by blood.

I agreed to stay and help them move Ajsa's stuff. Karim looked relieved. His chastity was no longer under threat by the dangerous and decadent sex, I supposed.

Ajsa was thinner than I remembered her. The crow's feet around her eyes, the slightly cavernous look on her face, accentuated her surprising leanness. Was it because the weather had removed some extra layers of clothes from her, from all of us? Or had she lost weight over the past few weeks?

Ibrahim did not come with her. He is out with Ali, she said, and shook her head. It was tightly wrapped in a black-and-white Palestinian scarf, her blonde hair almost invisible. Karim nodded, as if he understood. Later, I thought about that nod. I mentioned it to the police. The officer nodded too, as he jotted it down.

Ajsa declined to stay for a cup of tea. It took us less than five minutes to cart her boxes and belongings, some stored in the basement that we shared with all the residents, to the old blue Peugeot that she had borrowed from someone.

We had already been out as couples with Ms. Marx and Lena—once to a café and once to a French film in Øst for Paradis, the alternative theater in town. "You can tell it is alternative because you hardly ever see any Dane under fifty here," Ravi had quipped.

Now Ravi talked all of us into visiting Lena's parents for a weekend. Lena's parents lived in a village off Aalborg—very picture postcard, Ravi promised us—where they worked. It was just an hour's drive.

Ms. Marx had trouble fitting it into her schedule. Her son was going to his father only on Saturday afternoon. She could not leave before that. Finally, we decided to go first—Lena, Ravi and I—by bus. Ms. Marx would join us for dinner on Saturday night—she had a car—and I would return with her on Sunday afternoon. Ravi intended to stay on for a couple of days with Lena and explore, what he termed, her childhood shrubberies.

As usual, we asked Karim Bhai to drop us at the bus stop. Like most of our neighbors, we had got used to hiring his cab in the black. He always refused to let us pay, but then finally accepted a sum that was, as a rule, a bit less than his usual fare would have been.

That day, however, he refused to let us pay, perhaps because Lena was with us. Was it courtesy? Or was he just being careful with a Dane he did not know and who could inform on him?

Allah-hafiz, said Karim Bhai to us at the bus stop. Go in the care of God.

Allah-hafiz, Ravi responded.

Waiting for the bus, I took him to task. Lena looked on, bemused.

"Why the fuck do you have to say Allah-hafiz, Ravi?" I asked him.

"Why not, bastard? I say namaste, I say goddag, I say Merry Christmas..."

"It's not that. I remember you used to say khuda-hafiz. I distinctly recall you khuda-hafizing my parents with a vengeance when they visited three years ago."

"That was before Karim Bhai. He says Allah-hafiz."

"That is my point, you wannabe fundu! It was always khuda-hafiz in India and Pakistan: go with God, go in the care of Khuda, the Persian word for God. Now these woolly Wahabbis are trying to get all Arabic, and they insist on using Allah, the Arabic word..."

"Hardly an issue for me, bastard."

Lena did not know whether to smile or not. She never really understood the tone of our conversations around such issues: our disagreements and agreements were too uncertain and disorderly for her way of thinking.

"Yes, it is, you ignorant kafir. See, Allah-hafiz already existed as a phrase in Urdu. If you said Allah-hafiz, it was a dismissive gesture. Like 'Only God can put some sense in him now.' So these fucking fundus are messing up my bloody language, their own bloody language. It is a matter of historical and linguistic accuracy: Allah-hafiz does not mean the same as khuda-hafiz in Urdu, whatever it might mean in fucking Arabic."

Ravi mulled over the problem.

"Point noted," he said. Lena looked just a bit relieved; she took our arguments more seriously than we did. In general, like all the Danes I had met, she hated conflict of any kind. Revolution was not the only thing Tivoli had subverted, or so Ravi might have quipped once upon a time.

After this discussion, to be fair, Ravi went back to saying khuda-hafiz to Karim Bhai. But Karim Bhai either did not notice the switch or obdurately continued replacing the Persian "khuda" with the Arabic "Allah" in his responses.

Lena's parents had one of those flat-roofed, yellow-brick houses that appear to have been built in clusters all over Denmark during the 1970s. They are neither ugly nor attractive. They are convenient and nondescript. Like Denmark, Ravi would have snorted in the past. But flippancy was not on Ravi's mind when we alighted from the large Ford that Lena's "far"—dad—had driven to the bus stop to fetch us.

Far was tall and lean, impeccably dressed, with grizzled blonde hair: he spoke—no matter what the language—with such precision that it was easy to locate the source of Lena's drive for perfect poise and control. Apart from that, he did not resemble Lena. Mor—mum—was a broader and older version of Lena, but she exuded the kind of natural warmth that Lena lacked to my mind. No, Ravi would not agree with that. He always saw Lena as a person capable of more than she allowed herself.

We entered the house through the kitchen. It was large and comfortably furnished. The sitting room was big enough to contain two sets of sofas. There was a piano. There was art on the walls: mostly lithographs and watercolors. It was tasteful but not the sort of serious stuff that hung in Claus's flat: one had to be an art fanatic to have dinner under a painting by Michael Kvium, Ravi had once observed, and I agreed. A white PH artichoke lamp hung in the dining room.

It was the kind of house—comfortable, polished and predictably domestic—that would have elicited scathing comments from Ravi in the past. But he was on his best behavior now. He could not refrain from indulging in the occasional quibble, but he consciously avoided commenting on Danes or Denmark. I had never imagined him capable of such restraint.

After tea, we went for a walk in a neighboring forest—the trees had been planted in straight lines, crisscross, and Ravi could not help quipping that Danish forests were remarkably well-behaved. When we returned to the house, Ms. Marx had arrived. She was sitting in her station wagon, listening to the radio and waiting for us.

Ms. Marx and I were given the main guestroom, in the basement, while Lena and Ravi put their bags in the other guestroom, which had once been a sauna and still had florid yellow wood paneling everywhere. Ravi and Lena disappeared into the sauna-bedroom for a short while: they had not been alone for hours. All through the walk, I had noticed their hands fluttering like butterflies over each other, restrained only by the fact that Lena's parents were walking with us. In this, both Lena and Ravi were surprisingly conservative. They seldom kissed and never fumbled in public. But it was difficult not to notice how they automatically drew together as they walked, how their eyes swept each other relentlessly, caressing the sight of the other.

Dinner was cooked by Lena's parents. It was roasted duck in brun sauce, a Christmas specialty, which was the only meat dish Lena allowed herself. Ravi had offered to make something Indian— he had brought some of his powders and curries along—but Lena's parents would not hear of it. He was to cook tomorrow night instead.

"Why don't you two stay on, ba…?" he said to me, managing to stifle the customary "bastard" out of consideration for the sensibilities of Lena's parents. But both Ms. Marx and I had classes on Monday morning, and we needed to get back and prepare the next day.

What do I recall of the dinner?

Not much. It was a brilliant evening, probably: Lena and Ravi kept the conversation going, and Lena's parents were unusually well-informed and articulate. Ms. Marx, like me, is a quieter person; we needed to add only the odd bit of response or query. The food was good, the conversation was pleasant; the wine flowed. Ravi made a rare exception to one of his unspoken rules and played the piano—some lively Mozart, I assumed, though I have little knowledge of European classical music—with bravado and aplomb.

But what I really recall from that evening is something different. It took place after dinner. We had retired to the more comfortable set of sofas for coffee. Ravi, or was it I, brought up some reference to Baudelaire. Lena, whose French was as good as Ravi's, quoted a line in the original. Lena's father was uncertain about the pronunciation of a word. I do not recall the word; my French is not good enough to enable me to remember conversations in that language. But I recall Lena's father correcting her pronunciation and then, to be certain, consulting two heavy dictionaries.

It was a minor matter and it was done kindly, if much too efficiently, by her father. But for an instant, Lena looked panic-stricken. Her green eyes sought refuge in different corners of the room. There was only one other time when I saw her mask of confident poise slip—it was back up in an instant on both occasions—and that was to come much later, under circumstances easier to read. At that moment, though, as her father looked up the correct pronunciation of the French word, Lena glanced with something like fear at Ravi. It was as if she was afraid of falling in his esteem.

The next morning was Sunday and Ravi did something uncharacteristic. Despite his strictures against walks in nature on Sundays, he went out for a walk after breakfast with Lena and her parents. I tried not to smile.

"That was a very pleasant stay," said Ms. Marx, driving us back in her station wagon, after an early lunch. I agreed. I was too busy watching her steer to disagree with anything she might have said; I have always found it incredibly sexy to watch a small woman drive a large car. But I remember thinking that it was good Ravi was not with us: the word "pleasant" would have made him squirm. Or at least, it would have in the past, before he fell in love with Lena.

Great Claus was leaving Karim's flat when I got back. He looked irritated and almost forgot to respond to my greeting. Inside, Karim was obviously irritated too. I knew that Claus and Pernille often confided in Karim. I assumed they had disagreed about something. But I did not want to ask. I had a novel to re-read in time for my class on Monday. It was not a novel I wanted to re-read.

Sometimes I feel that there is a strict rationing of happiness by nature or providence or whatever you decide to call it. Some dark-coated bureaucrats sit there, dour and rule-bound, and flick the switch when light gets too abundant: let's cut the power, they grumble; let's ration the water, they whisper; time to switch off the happiness, they chuckle grimly. With Ravi's cup brimming over and mine around the halfway mark, which is all I have ever expected, a scarcity of happiness was to be expected in other quarters. The quarters where providence cut corners, for the sake of good governance, were those of Karim and Great Claus.

It strikes me that I am probably letting my current state of knowledge influence my narrative of those weeks to some extent.

But not entirely, let me assure you. I might not have noticed that Karim was going through a period of anxiety and restlessness, perhaps linked to those mysterious phone calls and disappearances. It might be that I noticed this about Karim only a bit later, perhaps as late as the Friday Quran session in which I had to intervene. But the unhappiness of Claus was quite obvious to all of us even then. He had lost his bounce. He dragged his feet up and down the stairs. He even forgot to greet us with his trademark "sob kuch teek-taak, na?"

It all came to a head a few days after Ravi got back. I could have ignored Karim's obvious irritation at Claus—he frowned every time the name cropped up in our conversations—but the aunties in Ravi would not be silenced. The glory of Lena's love had dazzled them for a while, but nothing could muzzle them for good. Soon they were busy working on Karim, mining for information. Karim was rocky territory. He was difficult to penetrate. But the aunties in Ravi had various tricks up their sleeves. Just when, after a few sallies, I thought they had given up, Ravi came up with the right approach. I am sure he still had belief in words as the key to all locks in those days: he must have been dying of curiosity by then, for it was a wild gambit.

Over dinner one night, as Ravi ladled out the shahi daal and matar paneer that he had painstakingly cooked, he said to Karim, "You see, Karim Bhai, there might be rumors."

Karim was too busy relishing the food to fully comprehend; he loved Ravi's cooking. He nodded, half-comprehending.

Ravi continued, matter-of-fact, as if he was discussing the weather, "Rumors, Karim Bhai. You see, people might think that Claus is unhappy because you and Pernille are having an affair, and that this is the reason why you and Claus do not get along any longer."

Karim dropped his spoon with a clatter. He always ate rice with a spoon.

"That is not true, Ravi Bhai!" he exclaimed. "How can you believe it?"

"Well, Karim Bhai," said Ravi, still as casual as ever, "you know people want answers and explanations, and you do not give them even to your friends..."

Karim Bhai slapped himself on his cheeks. This was the second time that I witnessed this traditional and theatrical act of contrition. Both times, I was surprised by the loud gesture; Karim was not a dramatic person, ordinarily.

"How can you say that, Ravi Bhai!" he muttered, his face a flaming red. I felt sorry for the guy; Ravi had been crueler than he was aware. Karim's Allah was not a very forgiving one. Surely Karim was wondering if Allah's angels trafficked in rumors too.

Karim turned to me and appealed to my estimate of his good character.

"You would not believe something like that?" he asked me. "Pernille is like a sister to me."

I shrugged. There were times when Karim's rigid morality, his conviction that Allah had personally penciled the flowchart of his life, made me feel cruel towards him. On such occasions, I wanted to shake him up as badly as Ravi claimed that he wanted to shake up the ordinary Dane.

Karim turned back to address Ravi, who was tucking innocently into the repast. Ravi ate Indian food only with his fingers.

"The Holy Prophet, peace be upon him, warned against talking behind people's backs. I do not like to gossip, Ravi Bhai," said Karim.

"Sure," replied Ravi, munching. "Sure. But others do."

"Not that it is something I cannot tell you," Karim continued, after a moment of hesitation. "Pernille and Claus have spoken about it to their friends and family."

Ravi continued eating nonchalantly, though I could sense the aunts in him straining at their leashes.

Karim hesitated for a few seconds more, drawing whorls in his rice with his spoon. Then he put the spoon aside, carefully this time. He lowered his eyes to his plate and disclosed the secret.

"You see," he said, gazing intently at his plate, for he was too embarrassed to talk about such matters while looking at us. Perhaps his Allah had injunctions about that too: an ayat or surah announcing that the correct way to gossip is to look intently into a plate of whorled rice and curry. "You see," he continued, "Claus has told Pernille that he wants a divorce. Pernille thinks he is having an affair, that he wants to leave her for another woman. She says she will never forgive him for that. Claus denies it; he says there is no other woman in his life."

"What do you think, Karim Bhai?" Ravi asked him.

"I think Claus is lying. I do not understand how he can do such a thing. I thought he was a decent man," replied Karim, shaking his head.

The matter took a further turn on a night when Karim had been called away by one of his mysterious phone calls. I recall it was a phone call, not one of his usual night shifts. I had picked up the phone. There had been a woman at the other end. The same voice. She had asked for Karim. As I knew she had trouble understanding my Danish, I had simply beckoned to Karim and handed him the receiver. He had spoken into it in monosyllables and muffled tones. He had left almost immediately, telling us that he was being called away on urgent business and would not be home the next two or three nights.

It was on the second night that Great Claus rang the bell of our flat. It was late. I had already put on my night clothes, and Ravi was lounging in the kitchen, TV switched on. He was probably whispering sweet nothings and translated poetry to Lena on his mobile, his almost-complete thesis languishing on the screen of his laptop.

We should have known that something was wrong, because Claus rang the bell. He was obviously too perturbed to knock, as he always did.

Ravi shouted to me to ignore the bell; we did not expect it would be Claus. But I went to the door anyway. Ravi was perhaps the only person in the world who could imagine that a shouted injunction not to answer the door, clearly audible on the other side, would serve its purpose. I was surprised to find Claus standing outside, in his slippers.

"Can I come in?" he asked sheepishly. "I need to borrow your phone."

Great Claus went directly to the phone in the lobby and pressed the numbers. He called Little Claus. It was difficult not to overhear or get the gist of the conversation between them; it lasted for at least ten minutes. It turned out that Pernille had kicked Great Claus out of their flat. She had done it with such determination that he had not had the time to put on his shoes or pick up his mobile or car keys. He was afraid of making her angrier by going back and asking for them. Instead, he phoned Little Claus from our flat to ask if he could sleep over. Little Claus agreed to pick him up.

Ravi had already brewed coffee in the kitchen by the time Claus finished his phone conversation and joined us.

Claus looked at us and shrugged, slumping into a chair. He knew we had overheard. He did not have to explain the situation. Perhaps he was even under the impression that Karim had told us more than he had.

Ravi brought him a mug.

"Shit happens," Claus said. He must have felt he had to say something.

Ravi turned a chair around and straddled it, joining us at the kitchen table.

"Shit happens," he agreed, "but sometimes we make it happen, Claus."

I was surprised that Ravi had decided to involve himself in the matter. He seldom took a stand on personal issues. Perhaps it was his relationship with Lena that made him care more about such stuff.

Claus did not say anything.

Ravi continued. "I think you should tell her, Claus," he said.

"Tell whom?" Claus either pretended not to understand, or he was too confused to focus.

"Your wife, Pernille." Ravi added, "You should give her a reason."

When Claus did not respond, Ravi continued: "You know your culture, Claus; it is a reasonable society we live in here in Denmark. How can you leave Pernille without giving her a reason?"

I looked at Ravi. In the past, a statement like this from him would have dripped with irony and sarcasm. But he was sincere that night. He meant it. Ravi was never flippant when faced with genuine confusion or pain—unless it was his own. He leaned on the back rest of the chair, facing Claus. "You have to see it from Pernille's perspective, Claus. You two have been together for years; you seem to share so much. Dammit, man, how many couples do you know who would agree to eat dinner under a Michael Kvium painting?"

Even Claus had to smile—wanly—at that.

"Now, suddenly, you want to leave her. Of course she wants to know the reason."

"It is not sudden," Claus mumbled. "We have discussed this for months, ever since the girls moved out..."

"That doesn't make it easier for her, Claus. She still wants a reason. If you do not give her one, she has to imagine what it might be. It would be kinder to confess that you are leaving her for another woman..."

"I am not leaving her for any woman," Claus interrupted decisively.

"Tell her the truth then. Whatever it might be."

"What if the truth is harder on her?"

"Believe me, Claus. It will be kinder than to leave her guessing. If you cannot tell her, get some friend to do so. Karim Bhai, for instance..."

To our surprise, Claus burst out laughing.

"No." He chuckled, actual tears of laughter in his eyes. "No, no... I can't see good old Karim telling her this..."

But then he collected himself. "I will think about what you said, Ravi," he promised. We started talking about other things.

Little Claus arrived within half an hour. He looked flustered.

The two friends hugged as if they were meeting after years. Then they left silently. We heard their footsteps going down the staircase until the main door closed and the silence surged back. It was late: the night was all wrapped up in itself. The twin flat upstairs was silent too.

LOUDLY SING, CUCKOO

Summer had partly gagged Ravi's criticism of the Danish weather in the past too. The most he could say was that you had to be attentive to derive the benefits of the Danish summer: you might blink, and it would be over. But the two weeks to two months that it usually lasts are, even he had to concede in the past, undoubtedly glorious. The sun is warm and the breeze still on the cooler side. The parks and countryside are dotted with yellow and white lilies, purple bellflowers, marigolds and a dozen other blooms I could not identify but Ravi could. The grass gets so uniformly and deeply green that, Ravi claimed, he was physically repelled by the color in his second summer in the land and almost threw up. It was too green, yaar; a bit like watching an obese man stuffing himself in a crowd of anorexics.

This summer, though, basking in the light of two Danish suns, he did not make too many quips like that one. Actually, on the train from Copenhagen to Elsinore that month, he relented long enough to praise the view. The sea rippled on one side, like a piece of parchment, crumpled and then carefully smoothened out, unbelievably blue.

The trip to Elsinore was Ravi's idea. Inevitably. Those days he was always coming up with ideas for visits and tours, most of which never bore fruit. Not all of us shared his disregard for schedules or his penchant for sudden projects and trips. This one we did take up, mostly because—for some reason—neither Lena nor I had been to the Kronborg castle in Elsinore. Set to patrol the sound between Sweden and Denmark—the cannons pointing at the sea had been good investment for centuries, ensuring toll collection by whoever controlled the castle—and built and destroyed a few times in the sixteenth and seventeenth centuries, Kronborg's claim to fame probably rests on the fact that Shakespeare made it Hamlet's castle.

"You have to hand it to Old Sheikh Pir," commented Ravi, as we lay down—a pause before descending into the dungeons—on one of the green slopes around the castle. Flocks of cloud scudded across the sky; seagulls drifted on invisible currents.

"Some cheek the guy had! He steals a story from someone, gets the facts mixed up and the time wrong, transports a prince from Jutland all the way to here and hatches a bloody masterpiece out of it. But, of course, he did not have you Eng Lit types telling him what to do in those days..."

Ravi was always good company; there is no doubt about it. Even Ms. Marx, who was not much given to flippant and dismissive remarks, would condescend to smile at some of his statements. But I have never seen anyone hang on his words and strive to match their brilliance as much as Lena. During that trip I wondered whether she did not, at times, feel a bit tired, that she did not sometimes feel that she had to let go, relax, not be so brilliant and poised all the time. Why didn't I feel that about Ravi? Why did I feel that for him it wasn't a strain? Was it because he allowed himself those moments of weakness, blankness and nonsense that Lena never revealed?

In the dungeons below, he paused in front of the muscular statue of Holger the Dane, his Viking head resting on the hilt of his sword. "Look!" Ravi proclaimed to Lena. "The Danish national hero: dreamed up by a Frenchman, fought all his life for the Germans, came back to Denmark and, guess what, immediately fell asleep forever."

Lena laughed. Even in the dark, rough, echoing dungeons, her laughter sounded like something that belonged in a room of china and tablecloths, its windows long and closed, its gossamer curtains slightly ruffled by the draft.

On the way back from Elsinore, we stopped for a couple of days in Copenhagen. As Copenhagen was known territory for all of us, we did not do much sightseeing, preferring to walk around and visit friends. Ravi did get us to go on one of those tourist walks, the one that takes you along the coast and past the Little Mermaid because, he claimed, he had failed to notice the mermaid statue when he last did the walk. "It's so bloody little," he offered as an explanation.

On our last night in Copenhagen, we did the customary pub crawl and ended in a pub we had not been to earlier, well after midnight. Even as we ordered drinks at the bar—sticky with spilled beer—we realized that this was not the sort of place we would have chosen to come to. It was full of young and middle-aged men—and almost no women—in various stages of drunkenness: Lena and Ms. Marx turned every pair of male eyes in the room. But it was too late; we were not even sure if other places were open this late.

I think Ravi and Lena noticed the atmosphere less that we did: they were too busy with each other. Even when a couple of men tried to chat up Lena—blatantly ignoring Ravi—I don't think they noticed. Lena, cold in her normal state, was icy with them. They returned to a group of rowdy, sullen men in their thirties at the back of the room, who were monopolizing the pool table.

A little later, another man from the group came up to us. Ignoring both Ravi and me, he asked Lena and Ms. Marx—in Danish—to join him and his friends for a drink. He was squat and sweaty; he had trouble standing straight. When he was politely refused, he turned and glared at us. Then he went back to the group around the pool table. There was some jibing and laughter. Then the squat, sweating man was suddenly back at the bar. He poked a stubby finger into Lena's shoulder. He zipped open his trousers and took out his dick. It hung half-limp, half-erect in his hands.

He said to Lena, in English this time, "Has your Italian boyfriend anything as good?"

I looked at Ravi, as both of us moved to get off our stools. I did so with greater reluctance than Ravi, I am sure. I disliked the option of regress to the caveman—always a danger in pubs full of men—though I also knew from experience that evolution is a fickle matter. Ravi, faster on the trigger in such matters, would have already landed a punch on the man, if he had not been on the wrong side of Lena.

But Lena anticipated it. In retrospect I could not help admiring her calm. She held up a hand to stop Ravi and turned to the man, who was suddenly looking just a bit foolish, with his dick hanging out and half the room staring at him. She looked him in the face for some calculated seconds and said, cold and collected as always, "Why, that thing! I wouldn't even feel it."

Swiveling again on her stool, she returned to her drink, turning her back on him.

The man looked bewildered. Ravi was off his stool now, ready to intervene if the man reacted violently. Then the barman, who had moved closer to us, started laughing. Some other people in the room followed his example. The squat man looked around. I think he decided that the laughter was not mocking; it was largely friendly, the sort of laughter a beloved clown evokes. Perhaps it was. Perhaps he was the resident clown, not the resident caveman, as we had assumed. He swayed, mumbled, tucked his dick away and shambled back to the pool table, where some of his friends were chuckling too.

Lena raised a thin, perfectly sculpted eyebrow at Ravi. Ravi winked.

Apart from this last-minute drama, I have good memories of our vacation together. I think of this brief summer as one of those periods one harkens back to as one gets older, a time when the sunshine was full of hope, the breeze whispered of happiness. All of us have such periods in our lives.

Perhaps it was the Danish summer; perhaps it was the radiant aura of love that wrapped Lena and Ravi. Once again, I could not help feeling that as a couple, in corny phrasing, the two were made for each other. Others must have thought so too: total strangers would turn and smile at them on the streets; bored waiters would smarten up to serve them with grace.

Ms. Marx agreed with me, but she also had her reservations. Ms. Marx had, by then, grown a bit skeptical of what she termed Ravi's "influence" on me: you two are not all that similar, she had told me, but when you are together, you start acting and talking as if you are Ravi's twin. I feel she underestimated both our similarities and differences.

Later, when we discussed the trip to Elsinore and Copenhagen, she complained about how difficult it was to travel with Ravi.

"He always tries to pay for everything," she said. "If you don't watch out, he pays for your drinks behind your back. After some time, you hesitate to order anything with him around." That explained the moments when she had seemed slightly irked with Ravi. Not Lena, though; if she found Ravi too quick on the trigger of tabs, she never betrayed it.

Yes, I already knew that Ravi liked to pick up tabs. He had offered to do so in Århus too, sometimes even if it meant that he had to walk back to the flat instead of catching a bus. But I had never found it excessive; I felt he was "Western" enough to curb such "Oriental" gestures when he needed to do so. Had he lapsed, in his love for Lena? If so, why hadn't I noticed it? Both Ravi and I were aware of this as a cultural difference in Northern cultures. We knew (without being fully conscious of it) that Ms. Marx and Lena, like all our Danish friends and colleagues, always paid for themselves and seldom offered to pay for others. It was not that they were tight; their generosity was occasioned and premeditated. There was just no excess to it. It was another kind of generosity, or so I felt.

I mentioned this to Ravi in his last weeks in Århus, those long November days so different from these days of summer.

"Nonsense, yaar," he retorted, "generosity is always in excess."

Strangely, I have almost no recollection of our return journey to Århus, but then that could have been because all of us—except Karim Bhai, who hardly commented on it—got preoccupied by the "Norway attacks," which took place that very afternoon. Ravi, in particular, did not hide his disgust at the ease with which many in the Danish media first blamed it on Islamists and then, when it became clear that a white, right-wing, Christian fundamentalist was behind these acts of terror and genocide, somehow still managed to suggest at times that immigration and Muslims were the real cause. He tried to discuss this with Karim over the next few days, but Karim Bhai just shrugged, sad, unconcerned or guarded. It was something I mentioned to the police officers later on.

I do remember that Ms. Marx left us at the station, as her row house was in the opposite direction, while Ravi and I took a bus to Lena's place—mostly to help her carry her luggage—before going on to Karim's flat. I recall that we remained on the pavement. Ravi handed Lena her suitcase, which he had been carrying for her. I lagged behind a bit to give them some space. They kissed, very decorously, a surprisingly proper peck on the lips. Then Ravi said to her, softly, though his voice—unintended—carried over to me by one of those quirks of the wind, "Will you wave to me before you go in? I always like it when you do."

Lena looked surprised and grateful. The ice of her poise cracked for just a micro-second: in that instant, she betrayed the sort of gratefulness that Ravi sometimes displayed in her presence. It was as new to her as it was for Ravi. But there was no doubt in my mind that both of them were grateful for and surprised by each other's love, or perhaps just by the fact of love. As if they could not believe their luck. This was not the first time that I noted how they parted. It was as if every parting, the shortest separation, was forever. Perhaps that is why Ravi wanted her to wave.

Lena opened the door of her building. Just before going in, she turned and waved. It was only then that Ravi started walking away.

What else? What else do I recall from that period? The torrent of the past seeps through the sieves of our memories and we clutch at the silt that sticks, trusting that it contains gold. Perhaps it does; perhaps not.

I recall lying in bed with Ms. Marx soon afterwards; we had just made love. Somehow, I don't remember why, we ended up talking about the scene in the pub, when that drunken clown had flashed at Lena. I must have praised Lena for her poise and her perfect put-down.

To my surprise, Ms. Marx was far less impressed.

"Ah, you men are such boys," she scoffed, reclining on the pillows, her forehead still slightly beaded with sweat. "Can't you see that poor Lena lives on male attention? All her perfection and poise is an index of her desperate need for it. She expects men to compliment her or flash at her!"

I felt that was unfair to Lena, but I dropped the topic with a laugh. You do not defend another woman when lying in bed with your girlfriend. I was not such a boy as that.

Despite that remark, Ms. Marx and Lena were always friendly with each other. It was also obvious that they would never be good friends. They met because of Ravi and me; left to themselves, they would not have gone beyond a polite hello or a coffee with university colleagues, I suspect.

The one person who had trouble being even friendly with Lena on the very few occasions when she visited us was Karim. He always got even more stiff and formal in her presence, and often left the flat abruptly. In my memory, I associate Lena's arrival in our flat with Karim's retreat, often abrupt, to his room or to the cab that would then start with a cough and a grumble and drive away. Was it her beauty? Was it because Ravi, to use a cliché, had stars in his eyes when he was with her, at least in those weeks? Was it the fact that Lena always dressed a bit too smartly and flamboyantly for the Islamist in Karim?

I never found out. Despite my lingering suspicion in those days that his Islam did not hinder Karim from frequenting prostitutes, it was never easy to talk about women, flippantly or seriously, in Karim's company.

WHEN AUTUMN LEAVES START TO FALL

One of my cousins was getting married in Lahore that August. August is not the best time for marriages in Lahore, but then the seasons have very little to do with weddings in the professional classes of Pakistan and, if Ravi is to be believed, India any longer. There was a time when there used to be marriage seasons, which varied a bit from community to community, region to region. Now, with jobs and education scattering the supposedly privileged all over the globe, weddings are usually crammed into the summer and winter vacations across the subcontinent.

Ravi had been talking about going to Pakistan with me, but that was until a few months ago. I knew he had no desire to leave the vicinity of Lena now. I made a quick one-week trip—sandwiched between the interminable sham-exams that cut into all vacations in Danish universities—and returned to find Ravi waiting for me at the airport.

I was touched. Ravi hated receiving or seeing people off at airports or railway stations. But no, Ravi was there primarily because he had news for me.

"Karim Bhai is in a foul mood: don't even mention Great Claus to him. He is liable to blow a fuse if you do!"

On the way back by bus—the airport is half an hour out of town—Ravi filled me in. It had to do, at least in his account, with Ravi's advice to Claus. Claus had followed the advice. He had told Pernille the truth. Pernille had been relieved; Karim Bhai had been scandalized.

"The closet," Ravi expanded. "Claus hath taken a mighty leap into the roaring Chandrabhaga!"

There had been no woman involved. It was more convoluted—or simpler—than that. Years ago, after he had fathered two daughters, Great Claus had discovered that he was gay. For years now, he had had a steady lover: Little Claus. There was nothing to be done about it. Great Claus felt he had to maintain the pretence of being a solid "familiefar"—family father—as long as his girls were too young and at home. But when they moved out, he could no longer keep on playing the part. He wanted to move out and become what he considered himself to be.

Pernille, Ravi said, had taken this revelation very well. She had even gone out eating with both the Clauses, and had helped Great Claus move most of his stuff into Little Claus's suburban house. The daughters too had been, if anything, jubilant about this turn of events. "You see, bastard," said Ravi to me, as the excessively green and even Danish countryside started giving way to a bit less green but as even Danish urbanity, "having an affair with a woman is kind of tacky and underhand. But who, with his heart in his left breast, can deny a man his true individuality! I wonder why good Old Claus hesitated in coming clean: the guy obviously does not understand contemporary Western civilization."

It looked like Karim Bhai did not understand it either. When Claus came to tell him, with both Little Claus and Pernille in tow, Karim Bhai looked shocked. "His face drained of color, yaar," recounted Ravi, who was there, all his aunts in tow. "I thought he would faint. Then he got up, walked to his room and closed the door."

"That is so stupid, Ravi! You should talk to Karim. He listens to you," I told Ravi, though even to me this advice sounded hollow. I felt angrier at Karim than I could convey to Ravi, for I suspected Karim of double standards regarding his relations to women.

"I did, bastard. You know what he did? He fetched his Quran and read out a surah to me. I can still recall the words almost verbatim. It went a bit like this: 'If two men among you commit a lewd act, punish them both. If they repent and mend their ways, let them be. God is forgiving and merciful.' End of discussion. He refuses to say anything more, or just stalks off. So, bastard, keep off all main and subordinate Clauses in his company for the next few weeks, parse your phrases, will you, Teach?"

But Karim Bhai was not home when we got back. He had been called away once again: he had left a note in his careful handwriting, telling us that he would not be back for a couple of nights.

Karim looked so tired and worn out when he returned that we decided to wait a bit before confronting him about his homophobia. Also, by then Ravi was less concerned with Karim's reaction, and more bemused by what he called "our failure to read the signs."

"How did we fail to spot it, bastard?" Ravi said to me at least twice that day. "It was so bloody obvious!"

"Are you teaching today?" asked Ravi, as he gathered up a few odds and ends on his way out of the flat on a Tuesday morning. From the way he was dressed, the subdued but clear hint of expensive aftershave that he exuded, and the careful disorder of his long hair, I could tell that he was on his way to the neighborhood of Lena.

"Yes," I replied. "*Wuthering Heights*."

"Ah." Ravi paused in his gathering of odds and ends. He could not ignore this opportunity to comment on literature; he seldom did. I often wondered what perverse impulse had driven him to do a doctorate in history rather than literature, except, of course, when he commented on what he called "Eng Lit types." The impulse always clarified itself then: The only time his voice dripped more sarcasm was when he commented on surgeons.

"Bet you a hundred you are going to give the standard poco take on Heathcliff, and your colleagues and most of your students are going to file it away as a quaint little notion, something that justifies your presence as multicultural artifact number one, though they won't say or even quite allow themselves to think so," he continued.

"What is the standard poco take, Ravi?" I asked him, though I already knew the answer.

"You know: Heathcliff as lascar; Heathcliff as a blackie, etc..." He held up a finger to preempt my response. "Yes, yes, I know what the text says, and sure I buy that reading. It is just, kind of, so obvious. Only whities could have missed it for close to two centuries. You know, bastard, most whities wouldn't notice a wart on the top of their nose if it happened to be black, which inevitably creates darkies who can spot a black hair on a polar bear at the distance of five kilometers. But the point of Heathcliff and *Wuthering Heights* is not really all that. Never underestimate a gal like Eternal Emily..."

"Enlighten us, O Great Critic," I responded, as he probably expected me to. Not that Ravi needed any encouragement from me.

"See, the problem in that novel is the problem of love: how, if it is really love, it is destined to fail in our world. This is not due to machination or enmity or other such humdrum matters, as in the weaker plays of your Billy Great Shakes. This is in the nature of love, which exceeds and challenges the order of our world. Hence, the only time it can come close to realization is in the wild, not in society. Finally, Heathcliff and Cathy haunt the sublime heath, while the rest of us go for walks in beautiful parks..."

Looking back and recalling this conversation, I realize that I should have suspected what was to come. But we are always wiser in retrospect.

As we could not possibly invite the Clauses to our flat without seriously inconveniencing our host and possibly the Clauses, we decided to ask Great and Little Claus to join us for an evening out in town. Ms. Marx was supposed to come too, but her babysitter absconded at the last moment and she had to cancel.

We met in a German "biergaarten," a place of much wood and heavy beer mugs. The Clauses were already there when we arrived. Great Claus had regained his bounce: his booming "sob kuch teek-taak, na?" had people at other tables turning around and looking at us when we entered. Ravi replied in Hindi, which of course Claus did not understand but pretended to.

Lena joined us but left early: she always had a busy schedule. However, even in that short while, she managed to fascinate the Clauses: her poise and beauty were of the sort that obviously left an impact even on gay men. Great Claus had already met her, but this was the first time Little Claus was meeting her, and he did not hide his admiration. After she left, Little Claus remarked, partly as a compliment to Ravi, that Lena was his notion of a really beautiful woman.

Ravi thought about it. Then he said, "Have you seen Waheeda Rehman, Claus? Say, in one of those Guru Dutt films? Now that was a woman who could manage to seem beautiful without being either showy or cold. That is difficult. I have never met a woman like that in real life."

Once again, I recount this little episode with the dubious benefit of hindsight.

There were three identical envelopes in the mailbox early that October. They were addressed in the same handwriting. I gave the one addressed to Karim to him, and went into Ravi's room to hand him his envelope. The third one bore my name. There were other letters, and a couple of journals for Ravi and me. We took the lot to the kitchen table. Karim Bhai was already there. He had opened his envelope and was now ripping it into vehement shreds. He was very intent on it. We watched him, a bit surprised. He threw the pieces in the garbage bin under the sink and left the flat on his way to work.

Ravi looked at me and said: "Claus?" He was right.

We had all received invitations from the two Clauses and Pernille: they had planned an early Christmas lunch—in November. The lunch was their attempt to broadcast their new status, and the fact that it was acceptable to everyone concerned.

It was obviously not acceptable to Karim.

Jul—Christmas—starts sometime around mid-November in Denmark, when the shops and streets get decked out for the season and a trace of frenzy can be detected in the activities of shoppers. That is also when the first julefrokosts—Christmas lunches, which are often actually dinners—are organized. All offices and institutes have at least one, and then there are those thrown by friends and family members, some of which have had the same patterns and participants for decades. When I first moved to Denmark, where places like Pakistan are considered traditional, I was surprised by how many traditions structured, sometimes rigidly, the lifestyle of the Danish middle classes. The Pakistani middle classes have nothing comparable, and neither—it seems to me—do the English middle classes.

Even people like the Clauses, who in many ways were as alternative as one could be in Denmark, participated in traditions like that of the annual julefrokost. And this year, they participated even earlier than usual. Their julefrokost was fixed for a Friday in early November. At first, I thought that it was due to their impatience to demonstrate their new status. I realized later that there were other factors: Great and Little Claus had taken three months off from their jobs and were going to work for an NGO in Kenya around mid-November. Pernille was to visit them with the girls for Christmas. Hence, the early julefrokost.

Ravi had been trying his best to make Karim attend the julefrokost. Karim had refused adamantly. I doubt that he would have gone anyway: consumption at julefrokosts can be tallied more in liters than in grams. But Ravi thought Karim's refusal had to do simply with his homophobia. That Thursday, as we had dinner together, Ravi even tried one of his maverick subterfuges: he suggested to Karim that the Clauses were not really gay; they were just pretending to be so in order to ease matters between Great Claus and his family.

For a moment, I thought Ravi's gambit would work. Karim took it seriously. He paused plying the mutton (halal) biryani Ravi had cooked splendidly in a bid to mellow Karim, and dangled his spoon in thought. Karim took everything more or less seriously. But then he shook his head and his beard.

"No, Ravi Bhai," he replied. "It is not what they are but what they have told me that matters. Only Allah can see into the hearts of men; we have to go by their words. They did not have to tell me anything. But now that I know what they claim to be, I have to do what my Allah wants me to..."

"How the hell do you know what Allah wants you to do?" I could not help blurting out, though Ravi tried to hush me. That objection had been bottled up in me all the months we had known Karim; it had to come out some day.

"It is all in the Quran," Karim replied, suddenly on Muslim-automatic, at least to my mind. It's the kind of non-argument that frustrates me: a stubbornness that denies all evidence to the contrary, entire histories of not just textual exegesis but even Quranic commentaries. I could not let it drop.

"You know, Karim Bhai, that the Quran is written in a dialect no one has spoken for centuries or fully understands; that it contains unclear and even contradictory injunctions. How can anyone know exactly what that book means, even if it is the word of Allah?"

Karim looked at me steadily.

"That is where we differ," he said.

"Not just there," I added. "You probably believe in hell too..."

"Yes, I do. Don't you?" I think my antagonism had made Karim take more adamant a stand on his faith than he usually did.

"If I had to choose, I might believe in heaven. The heaven we make in our minds, through our knowledge of what is right and wrong. But hell, Karim Bhai? Like in burning flames, like in being punished for your sins and wickedness..." I scoffed.

Karim Bhai ignored me. He turned to Ravi, probably expecting him to be more sympathetic, and said, "I am the first person in my family to get a postgraduate degree. I did not study in the kind of schools and colleges you went to; my education has not taken me too far, but it has brought me here. I have not seen as much of the world as you have. But I have seen the good suffer and the righteous forsaken. I have seen selfishness and wickedness triumph in this world. Surely there must be hell and heaven, Ravi Bhai, for otherwise wickedness triumphs for eternity too. The poor and weak in this world lose forever... Surely there has to be a hell along with a heaven!"

"Perhaps we bear our own hell and heaven, Karim Bhai," Ravi rejoined kindly.

"Is that enough? Is it enough for the victims?" Karim asked. Even I thought that it was a question born of curiosity, not argumentation.

"Believe me, Karim Bhai," said Ravi, "it is worse." Then he left the table, dumping the biryani left in his plate in the garbage bin and putting his glass and plate in the dishwasher, as he always did. It was abrupt, even for Ravi. I thought he was just closing the discussion, preempting an argument between Karim and me. I have thought about it since, and now I feel that he had other, personal, reasons. Perhaps Karim Bhai was right: each heaven comes conjoined with a hell. Including the heaven of full glasses of love...

By the evening of the julefrokost thrown by the Clauses, we had given up on recruiting Karim. Ms. Marx was out too. She did not know the Clauses and you do not turn up with uninvited guests in Denmark, not even at a party thrown by two liberated gay men and an understanding ex-wife. Lena had met them a couple of times—and, as Little Claus had joined her band of admirers, she had been sent a separate invitation too. I had expected her to come, but just as we were leaving, Ravi informed me—I ought to have guessed from the slightly inferior aftershave he had splashed on—that Lena would not be able to make it. This did not surprise me. She always had a full calendar and I knew that she was practicing for a gig with her jazz band.

Little Claus had a large suburban house off Virupvej, not very far from Hjortshøj. It had obviously been a farmhouse in the past; fields stretched out behind it. What struck me first about the house was the playground appended to a side plot: a sandbox with a tree house, a large swing, and a slide next to it. For a moment I thought that Little Claus, like Great Claus, had fathered and reared a family before exiting the closet. But Ravi, whose internal aunts were already remarkably well-informed, corrected me. The playground had been constructed for Great Claus's daughters, about fifteen years ago, when Little Claus purchased the property. By then, the Clauses had already been lovers. It sounded romantic and sad, the way Ravi put it: this act of generosity by a lover towards the children who were the reason why his love might never be publicly acknowledged, and who were, after all, also the children of his rival.

Inside, the house was the opposite of Pernille and Great Claus's flat. The furniture was old, unmatched and ramshackle; the paintings of no major value. I wondered if Great Claus would find it comfortable moving to such surroundings. From town to the countryside; from yuppie style to farmhouse comfort. But that evening he appeared to be happier than I had ever seen him, and completely at home.

Have I written that Lena was a trained opera artiste and that she was the lead singer in a jazz band? If I have, perhaps I need to define those two facts a bit further. Lena had taken lessons in opera singing: she came from a musical family and her father had started sending her to these lessons from the age of five. But at the age of twenty or so, it had become evident to all that she did not have a future in opera. She had tone and balance and near-perfect pitch; she learned everything perfectly. But she lacked volume, both in person—she was delicately built—and in her voice.

It must have been then that she switched over to becoming a student of music. She still continued to take singing lessons and sometimes she gave singing lessons to kids. She also sang in that jazz band I have mentioned: they were booked to perform in public only four or five times every year, but they met and practiced for a few hours every week.

Though Ravi had been to a couple of her performances, I had not managed to attend any. The previous fixtures had coincided with exams or a date with Ms. Marx, or something like that. I knew that her jazz band was scheduled to perform in a café in Kolding late that November—I forget the exact date or day, though I think it was a Saturday—and so I drove over with Ms. Marx.

It was a nondescript café off the pedestrian street, slightly more than half-full, and I had expected to find Ravi there. We had actually planned to surprise Ravi and Lena by turning up. Lena was surprised and delighted to see us. But there was no sign of Ravi.

We found a corner table and ordered a bottle of white wine and some peanuts. When Lena joined us at the table during one of the breaks, I asked her if Ravi would be making an appearance later in the evening. She looked just a bit confused. "He might," she said.

But the night wore on, the number of guests diminished, the jazz and early pop numbers got repeated, and Ravi did not turn up. Lena's band was not bad: like Lena, all the band members were obviously hard workers. The music they created could not be faulted. Whether it was Billie Holiday, Anita Baker or Diana Krall, everything was rendered with precision and poise. But it lacked—though Ms. Marx thought I was being too demanding (Ravi-esque, she said, actually)—that extra element which could have made it memorable. The sound was clear, the lines sharp, but in its very perfection there was something missing—as if the souls of the compositions were trapped and stunted in the perfect bodies of their rendition.

We left a bit before ten, when the café started filling up again. Lena's band was to play until midnight. Kolding is an hour's drive from Århus and Ms. Marx dropped me at Karim's flat just before eleven.

Karim had gone to bed—his door was almost closed—but Ravi was in the kitchen, working on revising his thesis. He had printed out what he hoped was the final version. It was this that had kept him from Kolding: he was reorganizing a central chapter in which he argued that the only way to understand the monstrosity of Nazism was to look at the "normal" concepts of law and order that framed even non-Nazi discourses in the mid-war period. He spoke about it for a few minutes before asking me what I thought of Lena's singing.

"It was good," I offered. "Very poised."

"Everything she does is poised and good," rejoined Ravi. At that moment, I heard this as a drop splashing off that full glass of love that Ravi had been bearing in his heart, though now I wonder why I did not consider it a sardonic statement.

"Yes," I continued, feeling called upon to say something more, "one could hear her opera training. It is a pity she has given up opera."

Ravi was shutting down his laptop now. He paused in the act and looked at me.

"I don't know," he said. "Do you recall those lines by Harrison where he talks about why he dislikes opera? He puts his finger on what is the soul of opera, and it is that soul which frightens him. One cannot be an opera singer unless one is undaunted by that frightful soul of opera, the non-rational excess at its core; one has to be willing to let go and face the freefall."

Then, because he could see from my expression that I had no recollection of the lines, if I had ever read them, Ravi quoted the stanza from memory:

"What I hated in those soprano ranges
was uplift beyond all reason and control
and in a world where you say nothing changes
it seemed a sort of prick-tease of the soul."

He picked up his laptop and went into his room, leaving me wondering.

Karim Bhai was a meticulous person. He liked keeping things in place. His room was the most orderly of all the rooms in our flat; Ravi's was the most disorderly. But Ravi, I had noticed, had specific oases of order in his desert of disorder. The clothes in his wardrobe were always in a mess, jumbled up, and pulled out to be ironed— or half-ironed—only when required, but his toothbrush and shaving things had to stand exactly in the corner or on the shelf where he put them. His papers were always in a mess, but his books were carefully arranged—not alphabetically but by the year of birth of the author, so that his shelves gave you a fair idea of the history of publishing.

Compared to the books Ravi had in his soon-to-be-vacated office at the university and the room, Karim had very few. Not more than twenty or so, stacked in precise order in a cane bookrack at the back of his room. Like everything precious in the room, the bookrack was also kept covered, so that one could not read the titles of the books. I recall noticing this only during the last Friday Quran session that I attended in the flat.

No, "attended" is not the word. As usual, I had no intention of attending inane discussions about religious matters, culled mostly from a book written in an obscure Arabic dialect no one spoke any longer. Some of the subjects that exercised the intellects of Karim's gathering—like clothing or food restrictions—were so much out of tune with my experience and life that I wondered what made Ravi go back to Karim's Friday sessions time and again. At first, I thought it was due to idle curiosity. Then I assumed he continued to attend them out of courtesy to Karim and his guests, all of whom—with the exception of Ali—got along with Ravi and felt flattered by his interest. But finally I had to concede that Ravi derived more intellectual sustenance from the conversations than I could, perhaps because—not having grown up in a Muslim environment—he found some of the ideas and sentiments fresh or thought-provoking. I also suspected that Ravi was willfully blind to what I had increasingly come to see as the fascist face of Islamism. He hated that suggestion, and with good cause, for in the West, Islam itself is considered fascist or prone to fascism. Ravi objected to that. He argued that Islamism, because it considered Islam universally valid for all human beings, could not be fascist, because fascism was an ideology of ethnic, racist or nationalist exclusiveness.

He might have been right, intellectually. But what Ravi forgot was that Islam, like any other religion or even an atheistic ideology like communism, could be put to fascist uses, and that many Islamic fundamentalists—with their mobs and chanting, their whips and executions, their insistence on absolute obedience—behaved very much like fascists.

I recall the discussion that Friday had to do with an example of what I still consider fascism in an Islamist mask. But, of course, I was not part of the discussion. I was waiting in the kitchen for Ravi to finish. We were supposed to meet Lena and some other friends later in the evening: we had tickets to a jazzed-up version, its operatic airs replaced by pop songs, of *Lucia di Lammermoor*, which was playing at a local theater. By then it had started becoming clear to me that things were not going well between Lena and Ravi any longer—not because they had fallen out of love but because, in different ways, they were still too much in love. I think the two of them were trying to do what they could to make it work, and the theater outing was part of that endeavor.

As I waited for Ravi to finish, I heard the conversation take a nasty turn in Karim's room. It also took a political turn, which was unusual. In the past, Karim had firmly stepped in and stoppered the genie of politics from being released. But that Friday Karim was distracted—he had been called away on his mysterious trips too often in recent weeks and had been working a lot as well—or simply unwilling to interfere. I must add that the second interpretation came to me later, when I spoke to the police about this particular Friday discussion.

Do you remember that in April last year a fundamentalist Christian preacher in USA had "tried," condemned and burned a copy of the Quran, after a year of infantile posturing back and forth? The news had been covered with surprising restraint by the international media but somehow it had reached fundamentalist Islamic preachers in Afghanistan, who had then led a mob attack on some UN workers, resulting in a number of shocking execution-like deaths. I am sure you will recall that unnecessary tragedy, as good an example as any of how the worst draw sustenance from the equally bad across their over-dramatized chasms.

What you might not recall is that in November a small postscript—almost unreported by the media—had been added to this tragedy. A Pakistani man—a Christian—in a place near Lahore had been (wrongly) considered a relative of the American preacher. Their names, transcribed inaccurately into Urdu, seemed alike. He had been accused of having provided the American preacher with a copy of the Quran to desecrate. A mob had collected, a mullah had pronounced a verdict, and the poor man had been dragged to a field and beheaded. It was, in my book, another example of the kind of Islamist fascism that held much of Pakistan in thrall, largely because liberal Muslims were too busy defending the complexities of Islam from unfair and at times racist Western charges of fascism to be able to face the actual and glaring fact of fascism in Muslim societies.

Strangely, in April, not one of the Friday discussion groups that Ravi attended had brought up the controversy for discussion. Or I would have remembered. Even bin Laden's dramatic death in May had not been discussed, as far as I could recall, and the "Norway attacks" in July been mentioned only in passing. Why? Well, perhaps because Ali had not attended them, or perhaps because Karim had been more in control. (The other explanation—subterfuge—came to me much later, in the light of other events.) But this Friday in November, the beheading of the Pakistani Christian was mentioned by Ali, who had come over with three other men.

Was Ibrahim there on that occasion? Later, the Danish police officer asked me that question too.

I am not sure. There were four Somali-looking men, but I did not stay in the room long enough to properly observe them. The police officer seemed dubious and shook his head in disappointment when I said so, but it was the truth. Ibrahim might have been there; or perhaps he was not there. I do recall—and I told the officer so—that Ajsa was not in the room. She seldom attended these Friday discussions.

Let me give you a clearer picture of the setting. There was Karim's sofa-cum-bed in the middle. Usually, Karim would be seated on it, but this Friday he was too restless—he kept going into the kitchen to fetch snacks or brew fresh tea—and as such he had relinquished the sofa to Ali and his cronies. Facing the sofa in a half-circle were six or seven men—I don't think there was a single woman that evening—on chairs, mostly folding ones. A table with Indian snacks and tea was set in the middle. It also held Karim's copy of the Quran, wrapped in clean cotton, placed on a wooden pedestal with inlaid silver patterns. Next to the Quran rested Karim's necklace of beads.

How did the argument escalate? I am not sure; I was reading in the kitchen, not really paying attention to the babble. Suddenly, though, I heard shouting—Karim was in the kitchen brewing more tea—and rushed to the room, followed by Karim. Ali and Ravi were close to hitting each other. Ali always appeared close to hitting someone or the other, even the words he uttered were expelled with a blast, showering his interlocutors with spittle. But it was unusual to find Ravi worked up to that extent; he usually managed to cut people with a comment or a regal gesture. I later realized it had to do with the phase that Ravi's relationship with Lena had entered, leaving him more vulnerable than I had ever seen him, than—I am sure—he had ever been.

I stepped in and parted the two. Ali left immediately, followed by two of his cronies, shouting. I remember his parting words:

"Anyone who insults the Prophet, peace be upon him, should be killed. It is every Muslim's duty!"

(The police officer looked very pleased when I reported these words to him.)

Karim apologized to Ravi, but I had had enough and pulled Ravi out of the flat. We were early for our theater appointment—we had agreed to meet the others for a drink in a café—but Ravi did not resist. I asked him what had caused the outburst. What follows is his account.

"The evening was shaping up as these evenings usually do," said Ravi, as we walked into town. We crossed an election billboard featuring Pia Kjærsgaard and her smile, which, Ravi had claimed in the past, reminded him of a well-fed cat being nice to a juicy mouse. Behind her was emblazoned the legend: Der er en grænse. "There

121

is a limit." "There is a border." I think both Ravi and I grimaced at the same time.

Ravi continued: "But then Ali and his cronies referred to this Pakistani Christian who was beheaded. I think Ali was trying to justify the act and also wish it away. You know, bastard, how you bloody mullahs behave when something really bad is done by your fellow Muslims: you look around desperately for the CIA or Mossad or someone else with an agenda to blame it on, and of course half the time those blasted motherfuckers are involved in any case. But then something like this happens, and no amount of Quranic exegesis can dig up a CIA plot. So Ali, poor bugger, had no choice but to defend the crime. I was lost in my own thoughts and did not pay him too much attention, but then he started talking about how all Christians were in the pay of the West and how the West was xenophobic and anti-Islamist. One of the other men objected and said that he did not think that all Danes were xenophobic."

We paused to allow a sleek, well-groomed white cat to cross the pavement. It did not slink past. It was well-fed and unafraid.

"This is the kind of cat," said Ravi, "that would give me a taste for mishi kanka." Then he returned to his account: "I tried to give the matter a half-ironic turn and said something like, 'I agree: Danes are not xenophobic. It is worse than that. Danes worship the heathen idols of comfort and convenience. Anything, any idea, or person that reduces their comfort or convenience has to be shunned or exorcized. They mostly do not dislike strangers from far places; they simply find them uncomfortable and inconvenient.' Ali, of course, is incapable of understanding anything like that, and very soon he was shouting about those stupid Danish artists who had made cartoons of your prophet and calling for their death, and for some reason I got provoked... That's it, let's forget about Ali. He is a fool and a rabble-rouser."

"He is a bloody fascist," I could not help muttering.

"No," Ravi replied. "He is just a fool and a rabble-rouser. But let's hasten, good sir, to the café yonder, where we shall say good night till it be morrow." Then, in keeping with the sudden quasi-Shakespearean turn of his language, he quoted: "Shall we their fond pageant see? Lord, what fools these mortals be!"

At that time, I thought he was still referring to Ali and his ilk. Now, I am certain I was wrong. He was not thinking of Ali anymore. I doubt that he could think of anything other than what was actually troubling him: a glass full of love.

The glass leaked, for the first time, that evening. I had noticed the ripples on its surface in recent weeks, but I had never expected it to leak. Or maybe it did not leak; maybe it brimmed over.

We were in the café, about six of us, including Lena. We were talking of this and that, the usual small talk on such occasions. Lena was the very epitome of poise and grace, so much in control of her speech and gestures that it sometimes appeared as if she were reading out her lines. I think she always made a special effort in Ravi's presence, tried to be even more perfect than she usually was. I am sure she realized that it was the wrong way to go with Ravi, but she was either too uncompromising or order and poise were too deeply ingrained in her for her to express love in any other way. I think that is what must have set it off.

Ravi turned to her suddenly and said, with his usual abruptness in jumping from one topic to another, "Didn't you take riding lessons, Lena?"

If Lena was surprised by the sudden change of topic, she did not show it. She seldom showed real surprise; if it showed on her fine porcelain face, it was because she knew it was expected and proper.

"Oh yes, as a kid," she replied. "For seven or eight years. I was pretty good too. My mother insisted on it: she loves horses. I never really did and I stopped as soon as I could. I have not ridden since then."

"But you still know all about bridle and snaffle..."

For a micro-second, she looked mystified. "Y-yes, I think I do," she almost stammered.

"See," Ravi turned and smiled brilliantly at me, "lots of snaffle and curb, but very little horse."

Then he pushed his chair back so suddenly that it almost fell over and he went out. We could see him light up a Marlboro outside.

I avoided looking at Lena. I knew she was confused. I could sense her sadness. For the second time I saw her mask slip, her fear show. But then she tried to pull herself together and started conversing with all of us, almost her usual charming, smiling self. Was I the only one who sensed the fine lines of worry and loss that fractured her poise and control? You had to be very observant to notice how suddenly her green eyes would flicker—with something of the palpitation of a caged bird—towards the window outside which Ravi stood, his back to us, smoking. Why don't you get up and go to him, I felt like saying to her. Don't you hear it? The murk of the café was repeating it in a persistent whisper all round us, in a whisper that seemed to wither, hollowly, like sand falling in a glass: her name, her name, in his silent voice.

But I knew I couldn't say it; I knew she would refuse to understand me if I did. That was a dialect for times long gone. She would never run out, grab him by the collar and kiss him. I looked at her again. The doll's smile had come back, stapled to her face.

Ravi returned only when it was time for us to leave for the theater.

A few words return to me here; words uttered by Ravi around that time, I am certain, though I cannot recall the context. Did he drop in at my office, or were we talking in one of the canteens? Was he lounging about, in my room or his, skimming quickly through a book? Or was he rolling a cigarette with Karim Bhai in the kitchen?

I do not remember, but the words I recall: "Did I tell you when I decided not to play the piano professionally? Somehow my dad had fewer objections to Western classical music—it was compatible with a scientific career in his mind, if only because of Einstein— than to my becoming a journalist or studying art. But one day I knew it was not for me. That was when my third piano teacher told me I had perfect pitch. I knew then that I had no future in music. Perfection condemns you to glorious mediocrity. It is in the gap between your imperfections, honestly faced, and your desire for something beyond perfection that you can achieve genius. Perfect pitch, perfect life, perfect love—these are dead ends."

I will leave the rest of it out. It is not just families that are happy in the same way but sad in entirely different ways. So are individuals.

But I will mention just one more thing. This must have taken place in the first week of December, or maybe a bit earlier or later. It was the week in which Ravi finally submitted his PhD thesis. He told me one morning that he'd a dream which finally made him "understand."

Understand what? He did not elaborate.

He claimed he had never dreamed in Denmark before, that the moment he came to Denmark, he stopped having the few dreams that he used to have. You just don't remember them, I told him.

No, he replied, seriously, yaar; I don't think I have dreamed a single dream in Denmark before this one. Not even a nightmare. I suspect they have ordered dreams away in this country.

Ravi wrote down the dream, with some poetic license, as a short story. It was one of the stories he shared with me. A week or two later, he posted it on an open-access online site. He had never done so with any of his creative writing before, and he hasn't done so since, as far as I can see. Ravi was a book person. Online publishing did not mean much to him. If you Google him, this is the only open-access story or poem by him that you will be able to find. I think he wanted someone in particular to read it. Though sometimes I wonder.

He called the story "A State of Niceness"; it was narrated in the third person. The version that I have copied here is taken from that online edition.

But it was difficult to locate when I wanted to find it for inclusion in this account. I got a number of hits when I Googled "A State of Niceness." I had always considered it a brilliant title for a story set in Denmark. But, obviously, Ravi and I were not the only people to think so.

So much for originality!

I hit upon another story—published in print in several places but not accessible online—with exactly the same title. By a strange coincidence, this story is also by an Indian writer—a chap called Khair—who had lived in Denmark some years ago. I could not find a copy of Khair's story. I do not know if it shares anything with Ravi's story of the same title. Anyway, it is Ravi's story that concerns us, and that is the story I have copied in the next chapter.

A STATE OF NICENESS

The wipers made a slight sucking noise that Ravi felt at the back of his head. Maybe they made the noise only in his head. Surely that was the case: how could he possibly hear the sound of wipers brushing away the relentless autumn drizzle in a car that was hermetically sealed against the outside? It is something he never got used to: these sealed cars; windows up, always. No draft except the smooth artificial airflow of the air conditioner. Just warm enough. A smell like that in a room closed for too long, like a prison room, the smell of staleness deodorized to a nicety. But it persisted. Ravi smelled it in all such cars, Fords, Mercedes, Chryslers, cars so different from those, even when imported, that he had driven, windows down, wind ruffling his hair, in India.

A wall covered with Virginia creeper flashed past; it was blood red now. Autumn had entered the short phase, a few weeks between drizzle and barrenness, when an explosion of colors redeems the death to follow. But he was insulated against even that.

The car smelled of a stuffy niceness. Or did it? He could see his parents-in-law, both schoolteachers, both extremely nice people, sitting up front. His father-in-law, reasonable, sane, grizzled blond hair now gone a steely grey, was driving. His mother-in-law, reasonable, sane, blond hair still kept blond with the help of various lotions and dyes, was leafing through a sales catalogue. They obviously could not smell the stale niceness that pervaded the car. Ravi wished he could lower the windows or get out for a quick breath. But it was drizzling outside, and cold. It would be strange if he lowered the window. It wouldn't sound nice if he said he wanted to get out and breathe. Shout. He had been conscripted into niceness by his decision to stay in this country, his decision to marry here two years ago.

He closed his eyes and imagined his wife cycling to meet them. She was returning from her singing classes: she now taught singing in an adult education university, while she continued with her post-doc. Her parents, still living in the village near Aalborg where she had grown up, were passing through the city and had invited them out for dinner. Dinner at six. Sharp. That was another of the things Ravi had to get used to.

In his mind, he could see her cycling, wearing her smart brown raincoat, focused—as always—on what she was doing, busy, busy, busy. Her golden blonde hair was tied into a neat orderly bun. She had been less focused once, she had claimed, but then that period, if it ever existed, was before Ravi had met her. She was not doing a PhD in musicology then, let alone a post-doc; she had even had a breakdown of some mysterious sort. Ravi could not imagine her breaking down now: she was always so much in control. He wished he had known her then. Then, when she had spent a couple of years dabbling in the humanities, a relationship to time and degrees that Ravi, coming from a country where careers were aborted by a single lost month, would have failed to understand if he himself had not come from what his Maoist friends in India liked to call the filthy rich.

But even then, at the time when she was dabbling in the humanities, Ravi already had a career as a journalist in India. After an initial hesitation, which had lasted for almost two years, he had quit his job, spent a year in USA and then moved to this country to do a PhD in history. He had started off, like any other immigrant in West Europe, by earning extra money doing odd jobs, mostly menial work that could be performed by those who did not speak the language. His PhD had progressed slowly. He had finally finished it, though, and was now teaching in a high school. He felt he had drifted into something to which he was largely superfluous. This controlled world, the universe of his married life, this orderly state of niceness all around him, his own inability to be rude.

They must have SMS-ed or synchronized their watches. They had just parked the car and walked to the entrance of the restaurant when Lena, his wife of the past two years, cycled up and joined them. The restaurant was in a dour, late-nineteenth-century building, grey and solid. It looked more like an office building than a restaurant. But it was, Ravi knew, an expensive place, the sort of place frequented only by those who were in the know.

Past the flanking columns of the door, engraved into half-pillars, there was suddenly a darkly red-carpeted, sumptuous world. There were rows of coats, overcoats and jackets. A low, diffuse light burned overhead. To the right was the door to the hall of the restaurant, up three small steps. It exuded warmth.

Ravi could not follow his in-laws and Lena through the door into the restaurant because he was the last one in the row, and when he hung up his jacket, first Lena's jacket and then her mother's coat fell off the hooks on which they had been precariously and hurriedly placed. By the time Ravi had hung the jacket and the coat back on the pegs, Lena and her parents had entered the restaurant and disappeared in its artificial candle-lit gloaming.

Inside, at the reception counter, Ravi was stopped by a very Scandinavian-looking waiter—tall, broad, blond, even teeth cared for by state-subsidized dentistry from kindergarten onwards—who looked at him with some surprise. When Ravi's eyes got used to the gloom and began to register the other guests (almost all the tables appeared to be occupied), he could understand the surprise in the waiter's eyes: Ravi was perhaps the only dark person in the hall. I am meeting friends here, Ravi told the waiter and walked in. The waiter did not look convinced and might have intercepted Ravi, but at that moment some elderly ladies congesting a table beckoned for attention. The waiter moved in their direction with a dubious glance at Ravi.

Ravi was in a hall of wooden paneling and rich dark furniture. There were plain white tablecloths, thin elegant candle-stands, maroon or dark-green curtains. Everything was subdued and affluent, with the affluence of those who do not have to demonstrate their wealth or taste. It did not appear to be a particularly large hall to Ravi, but even then he could not spot Lena or her parents. They seemed to have disappeared, swallowed into this Aladdin's cave of taste. They fitted into its careful order so well that Ravi could not discover them anywhere.

Walking about in the murky light, Ravi felt odd. He felt he stood out: was it due to his consciousness of the difference of his skin or the difference of his activity in this place? He was the only person who appeared to be looking, and people who look around always seem a trifle lost. All the others were firmly ensconced in their places; they looked like they belonged there and when they moved they had a definite goal: the restroom, the door, the counter. The waiters moved about with just as much assurance and certainty. Ravi wavered in their midst, talking a half-step in one direction and a step in another, looking.

Then suddenly he caught sight of Lena. He knew she was not allowing herself to look for him; he knew that the orderly rules of this place required such control from her and, as always, she was going to exercise full control. The room appeared to have changed. It had opened up. It was more cavernous and much larger than it had appeared at first. For the first time Ravi realized that he could not tell where the hall ended. It stretched in front of him, rows and rows of polished tables, ironed tablecloths, people pouring wine, consuming dishes, conversing in low tones, politely.

There was something like a huge bowl further up, with ramps leading up to it from four directions. The bowl appeared at least a story high. He realized, with no sense of shock, that it was a salad bowl, with other small bowls ranged around it: great cornucopias full of fruit and salad. He had glimpsed Lena walking calmly towards it, along one of the ramps, heading for one of the platforms from which people helped themselves to the salad.

He needed to get out of the shadows of the section where he was standing. He needed to catch her attention, though she was not looking around for him. She did not look around too much for him anymore. He suspected that her love for him, which she claimed was more than anything she had ever felt for anyone else, had its own place in her orderly life; one only looks around for things that have been misplaced.

Ravi realized that the section where he stood was a raised platform. The stairs were some way off. He could not reach them without losing sight of Lena. So he braced himself and, knowing it would draw eyes to him, jumped down from the platform to a lower level, a hop of three feet or less. All the diners around him turned and looked, precisely but briefly, perhaps even more briefly when they realized what he was, as if that explained his lack of etiquette, his jump.

But the jolt of the jump and the eyes turning to him had momentarily disoriented Ravi, and when he looked up, he could not spot Lena again. He stopped a passing waiter to enquire, but the waiter gave him a blank look and moved on.

Ravi was reminded of the lack that had crept into his relationship over the weeks. Or perhaps it had always been there; he had just become more sensitive to it in recent weeks. He missed the ordinariness of jerky gestures, the generosity of disorder: their relationship had always been too smooth, too fluent for him; things had fallen into place too easily.

This craving for clumsy, vulnerable things: the potted flower in the wrong corner, the striped curtain with a tear, the blackened pot simmering in the kitchen, the novel on the sofa, the crumbs of toast on the table, the voice raised in indecorous and joyous greeting, a spontaneous unpremeditated gesture. How easily Lena could have extended these to him, how steadfastly she refused to do so. Not out of cruelty or lack of love but because she took the normality of order and control for granted. She had grown up in a nice world. She had not had to constantly gather up fragments of the ordinary, the daily, in newly broken settings.

He felt it was like that with almost all of them, despite their concern, despite the niceness. And it was buttressed by a belief that, after all, they lived in the best of worlds—and any of his losses were amply compensated. The losses had to be acknowledged at times, but only at a hidden personal level, never as a matter of the world, a flaw that increasingly appeared structural to him, a way of life. What difference could even his rich childhood make to this structural flaw in the world? Never here, never with Lena, he feared, would there ever be a public acknowledgment of the right of loss, pain, disorder to be and to be freely expressed. It was also simply taken for granted that coming from where he did, being what he was—westernized, professional, irreligious—it was natural for him to seek to be here. And, as such, he felt, it was always him seeking (and often not finding); it was always he who had to move around, make space, look, ask, hold.

Tired of asking and looking around in a place that seemed without end to him, Ravi gravitated back towards the section near the entrance, the exit. He stood next to a table lined with national newspapers, with editorials worrying about the state of the world and making polite noises of criticism about the treatment of refugees in the country, and tabloids full of lurid scandals and crimes, the latter often pointing a vague finger of accusation at immigrants. He did not necessarily disagree with all the newspapers and they did not always agree with each other, but Ravi found their assurance, whether it was about Nigeria or Denmark or USA, difficult to stomach. It was this commonality of tone that made all the news sound like a repeat of what Ravi had read for weeks, months, years. But just as he could not walk away from the restaurant—it would have been rude of him, surely—he could not resist reading such headlines day after day. They were in different ways (mostly well-meaning, mostly nice) so oblivious of him, and yet he had to keep looking at them, for them, these printed words he knew by heart even before they were printed each night.

He stood there browsing through the newspapers for five minutes or so. It was then that he noticed a corridor leading to a quiet and empty section.

The corridor had surprisingly cheap wooden paneling. The section it led to was empty, and unlike the rest of the restaurant, it had chairs piled up on the tables. The chairs and tables were of the spindly kind used in cafés. This section was probably used during earlier hours to serve customers who wanted a coffee and cake rather than a meal. Ravi walked into it listlessly, noticing the chairs and round wooden tables, the empty beer counter, the pattern on the floor.

He was looking at the floor when he almost bumped into someone. It was a waiter, not a local this time, but someone from the Middle East or Turkey. Can I help you, sir? the man said in English. A surprising feeling of gratitude flooded Ravi. He noticed that the man did not wear the uniform of waiters. He was probably a cleaner from the kitchens below, sent up to fetch the tray of dirtied utensils that he was carrying. Ravi explained his search to the man.

Have you looked in the reserved sections? asked the man. Seeing the look of incomprehension on Ravi's face, the man pointed to the cheap wooden paneling along one side of the corridor: there are rooms behind those panels. They are usually used by special guests. Your family might have been placed there.

Ravi slid one of the panels open, and was met with garish light. The room inside contrasted with the main hall of the restaurant through which he had been walking until now. The main hall was dimly lit; the guests were dressed in conservative greys, blue and black, the tables arranged at a polite distance from each other all over the floor. Pearls and silver hung from the ears or around their necks and sometimes glinted decorously in the candlelight. But this hidden room was like a wedding shamiana in a small town in India or Pakistan. It was garishly lit: the men talking confidently, the women speaking in low tones or keeping quiet. Some of them wore gold. There was a buffet table in the middle of the room, piled with dishes, and the chairs were ranged along the four walls.

This section was more disorderly than the other parts of the restaurant, but it was an abashed sort of disorder: as if a housewife had received unannounced guests and had done what she could to tidy up in a jiffy. As if order was the state that was being aimed at, and the bits and pieces, the napkin or crawling child on the floor, were inherently a failure.

Ravi realized with a shock that almost all the people sitting in the room, the women dressed in gorgeous colors, were South Asians: Indian, Pakistani, Bangladeshi, Sri Lankan. The women mostly sat on the chairs along the walls, holding plates of food in their hands or laps, sometimes feeding a child. The men, more conservatively dressed, stood conversing desultorily in groups all over this secret room in the paneling. They were attired like aspiring businessmen or government functionaries on a rare trip abroad. Some of the groups were mixed, but mostly the men stood together.

A thickset middle-aged man spotted Ravi and sauntered over to him. "You live here?" the man asked in a heavy Haryanvi or Punjabi accent. Ravi nodded in affirmation. The man's slightly florid features lit up with a smile and a smirk of recognition: South Asian to South Asian, Indian to Indian, man to man. So, where are the fun spots of this famous city? he asked again, with a wink. You know, he repeated, the fun places.

It took Ravi more than a couple of seconds to understand the question. Slowly the words sank in, reinforced by the sly look in the man's eyes. It was not really a leer. Ravi stared at him for another second. Then he did something incredibly rude: he turned on his heels and started to walk towards the exit.

NOVEMBER, NOVEMBER, NOVEMBER

The uncertain summer, rain-riven one week and sun-drenched the other, had hiccupped into a fluctuating warm and cold autumn that year. This was a relief, as there were autumn days when the annual darkness was held at bay. November really started in December, at least for Ravi. But it lasted, as Ravi's favorite Danish poet had prophesied, much beyond December.

I have looked at some of what I have written until now and I am surprised by the fact that it is my relationship with Ms. Marx that comes across as passionate, in an immediate sexual sense, while Ravi's glass-brimming affair with Lena, if one were to disbelieve Ravi's words, might strike you as restrained and cold. Perhaps that is so because I cannot really say much about Lena and Ravi. It is true that when Ravi spoke of his feelings, which was not as often as you might assume, or when—and this was quite often—he spoke of Lena, I had no doubt that his metaphor of the full glass was valid. Occasionally, when I saw them together, I would feel convinced too, but not always. There were moments when I resented Lena on

Ravi's behalf—because he seemed so incapable of resenting her—and wondered whether she shared the passion that Ravi felt. Or was she simply flattered by the flamboyance of his love for her? Ms. Marx had planted the germ of a doubt in my mind. Sometimes I felt that whatever Ravi saw in her was just a reflection of his own fire, and what Lena was capable of was not passion but niceness.

Ravi must have had his doubts too, as his dream-story suggested to me. But his faith in Lena's love was never shaken. Looking back, I see this as something he had in common with Karim Bhai. Perhaps that is why they took to each other across such obvious differences of background, character and habit. There is obviously a very thin line dividing faithfulness from fanaticism—and I wonder if, in a world of easily exchangeable commodities, we can even see that line anymore. I know I could not in the case of Karim Bhai. Perhaps Ravi could. Perhaps Ravi thought he could. Perhaps that is why he never grew suspicious of Karim, on his own, not until I talked to him.

But there might have been something misleading about the way I narrated my relationship with Ms. Marx too; particularly, I fear, the kitchen scene. There are too many Hollywood films in which you see pans flying and plates smashed as the hero and the heroine bounce from one kitchen wall to another and finally end up enmeshed on the floor. I would be misleading you, reader, if I implied that this was the standard procedure between Ms. Marx and me.

Remember, Ms. Marx had a seven-year-old son. Even if we had been the sort that wished to bounce from kitchen shelf to kitchen floor, oblivious of either the danger from knives and jagged pieces or the expense of broken china, the presence of a young boy in the house would have precluded that option.

After we started seeing each other regularly—"became a couple," in common parlance—Ms. Marx had no objection to me sleeping over and, late in the night, engaging in what Ravi once described as the pre-conjugal act. This was to be done carefully, of course, with a towel spread under us, for the easy elimination of evidence. But the first night we did so, just when the towel needed to be straightened, Ms. Marx's son knocked on the door. It was eleven. We were under the impression that he had been asleep for close to an hour; Ms. Marx had worked hard on getting him to fall asleep, despite an obvious reluctance on his part, most of that evening.

Hvad er det nu, asked Ms. Marx, struggling to get back into her nightdress and keep irritation out of her tone.

He had had a nightmare, he claimed in a small voice.

Ms. Marx had to spend another half hour putting him to bed. When she got back, she was willing to roll out the towel again, but I dreaded another knock. I could not get rid of the image of a young boy pretending to sleep in his room, trying to avoid hearing those telltale sounds that, no matter how careful we tried to be, he could not avoid hearing in a small place, sounds that would be more disturbing to him because he could not really understand them. The pragmatic attitude that so many Danes, including Ms. Marx, have to these matters was not something I shared to such an extent. After that, we confined our love-making to periods when Ms. Marx's son was staying with his father.

And yes, in case the image of a kitchen of bouncing pans and cascading plates still arises in your mind, let me add one further clarification: the towel stayed in place.

If Ms. Marx was disappointed in me as a Muslim, she tried not to show it. This was always a source of hilarity to Ravi, who urged various disguises of Muslimness on me for, in his words, the sake of good form.

Ravi could be very explicit in his curiosity and comments at times, though never without humor; in this too, he differed from Lena.

For instance, the evening he brought up circumcision. We had finished our dinner and were lingering in the kitchen. Karim Bhai and Ravi were smoking. I don't think Ravi had smoked that day—he did not really like smoking—and so he had to light up before going to bed, simply to keep protesting against the Danish establishment's anti-smoking policies on the behalf of women and the working classes.

The nicotine must have sparked some neurological circuit of needling in his labyrinthine mind, for he paused between puffs and said, "Sometimes I feel I should have introduced Ms. Marx to Karim Bhai here; he would have been less disappointing."

Karim Bhai looked alarmed, not following the conversation but gathering that it had to do with women. I ignored Ravi. I was watching TV.

He continued, "You know, Karim Bhai, I suspect the bastard here is not even circumcised!"

This was sheer nonsense of the sort that Ravi was capable of spouting occasionally, but Karim Bhai trafficked only in sense. He looked at me, perturbed.

"Oh no, no, no," he replied to Ravi. "All Muslims are circumcised. It is written in the Hadith."

"I betcha this Paki turncoat ain't!" Ravi maintained, not realizing that Karim was taking his needling seriously.

Karim Bhai turned to me for confirmation.

I gave up. I knew this would go on unless I set Karim's mind at rest. Ravi would turn his idea into various other avenues of jocularity, unaware of the truck of Islam careening out of control in Karim's mind. It was then that for the first time, fleetingly, I noticed a slight trace of bitterness—of disappointment, perhaps—in Ravi, which sometimes made him needle his friends. The reason was not difficult to guess. It was his brimming glass of Lena.

"Of course I am circumcised, bastard," I replied.

"You mean, the proper way, when the barber seats five-year-old Munna on a stool, razor glinting, and says look look look a silver bird in the sky..." Ravi did not want his joke to deflate so soon.

"Know what, bastard," I told him, "you are worse than the RSS: everyone goes to hospitals now. No one is circumcised like that anymore."

Karim Bhai was smiling. I think he was so relieved to be assured of my Muslimness that he overcame his shyness about physical matters. "Not true," he said to me, "I was taken to a barber, you know, silver bird and all..."

He went pink to the roots of his beard.

Let me try and be fair to Lena. I know my vision of her is clouded by the pain that I thought I detected on Ravi's face, the hollowness in his heart that he struggled to hide and almost succeeded, those weeks when his hands were hummingbirds hovering over the flower of his mobile. To be fair, Lena is the only Dane I have known—apart from the Clauses who were always consciously "Asian" with us—who was infallibly courteous. This has to be put on record, I think.

Even Ms. Marx can be quite brusque, in a typically Danish way. I recall, when I first moved here, I had found the Danes an incredibly rude people. So had my ex-wife. I still find them rather rude. But I think I understand it a bit better now. It is not just the "unholy alliance of capitalist pragmatism and subterranean Protestantism," as Ravi used to put it. It has to do with the myth of honesty that structures Danish society.

Look at it this way. Your Danish friend Mr. Xyzsen asks you to do something for him and, without telling him, you go out of your way to oblige. Mr. Xyzsen is happy but he does not feel obliged; he assumes that you did what you did because you too wanted to do it at that moment. Otherwise, surely, you would have refused. So when you ask Mr. Xyzsen to do something for you, he declines—because he is too busy or simply not in the mood. He is just being honest with you, because he assumes that you were being honest with him in the past. But, of course, courtesy is basically a matter of dishonesty—you hide your own inconvenience in order to be courteous and, sometimes, kind.

Lena, though, as I wrote, was always courteous and kind in company. Was she kind to Ravi? It is irrelevant; I don't think he ever wanted kindness from her.

One night, late in that long multi-month November, as I lay on my back on the striped towel that we favored for the elimination of evidence, and Ms. Marx maneuvered marvelously atop me—her son was with his dad—the topic of Ravi and Lena came up. That is how I found out. Ms. Marx had a practical attitude to sex; she was capable of discussing anything from Norman Davies to the latest feud over the disposal of garbage among the residents of her housing co-operative until minutes before orgasm. So was I, to be honest.

That night, as she pinned the fundamentalist in me to a striped towel on her bed, she said, "You do know that your friend and Lena are not together anymore."

My state of sensation was obviously more advanced than hers at that stage; her remark did not register.

"Um, um," I think I replied. "Keep going, keep going..." She stopped.

That caught my attention.

"Your friend and Lena have broken up," she said.

"Bullshit," I replied, though actually I was not altogether surprised.

"Didn't you know?" she asked me, showing signs of moving back into gear.

"How do you know?" I countered.

"When did you last see them together? And in any case, everyone at the university knows it is over..."

She was right, as I realized when I asked around the next day. I still do not understand why I had not noticed, though I can understand Ravi's reluctance to mention it to me. After all, I was the only person to whom he had spoken of the depth of his passion for Lena.

To my credit, I did not ask Ravi about the break-up until, a couple of days later, he told me himself.

I can still recall that afternoon. It was the last time I saw Lena and Ravi walk together. Ravi had finally told me about their separation, though I had realized after my night with Ms. Marx that I had been rather blind not to notice the way Ravi kept looking at his mobile and checking his computer.

The break-up had been his decision: Lena had not demurred, he told me with a short laugh. She had accepted it with the kind of grace, equanimity and poise that she brought to everything in her life. I had felt like shaking her, he said.

But then that day, we bumped into Lena on campus. She was so collected and polite that both of us felt we had no choice but to walk with her to her flat.

To be honest, Ravi was just as collected, even perhaps a bit debonair, as if all those moments of frantically grabbing his mobile had never taken place.

The sky was overcast, almost dark, though it could not have been much past four. With the first snow yet to fall, winter was just a watery waste. Lena and Ravi did not say anything of significance to each other. They said very little of significance to me either. Instead, they kept up a fragile shiny prattle that at times I hated both of them for. If ever there was a couple painfully in love and determined not to show it, it was them. Or is it that I had been too influenced by Ravi's perspective on the matter?

When we reached the building, Lena said goodbye to us. She looked fleetingly at Ravi, and Ravi, who had been observing her a moment earlier, drinking her in with his eyes, managed to look away at that precise instant. As if each had coordinated his or her gestures in such a way as to avoid, with perfect timing, the other's moment of weakness. Then we stopped on the pavement and Lena walked on to her building. She walked straight, steps as measured as always. She opened the heavy door of the building. The door was blue, its paint peeling, wood warped and scratched: it made a contrast to Lena's youth and immaculateness. Just before going in, she half-turned. She did not wave.

It was only then that Ravi started walking away.

I had expected Ravi to do a repeat of what he used to do after his earlier break-ups: hit the bar, do ironic renditions of Mumbai film classics—Bombay, he would insist, as he refused to use the word "Mumbai," attributing it to what he called Sena bullying—and have to be lugged to bed. But no, he hardly drank in the days left to him, not more than a glass or a couple of beers; he preoccupied himself with clearing out his office and other such practical matters. He read a lot and even wrote a bit. He called up old friends all over the globe and had bright, witty conversations with them. He still looked at his mobile too often, but that was the only slip. And once in a while, though always abruptly, he would say something about Lena.

"Words, words, words; she is so good with words!"

"So are you, Ravi."

"Not in the same way, bastard. I do not trust words. No Indian does. Words leave me famished; I eye them with suspicion. Language is, first of all, a weapon. Man became the deadliest of all species when he invented language. If dinosaurs had survived until then, wordy *Homo sapiens* would have had them for breakfast! I could give up all words for one significant gesture: the breaking of bread, the offering of a glass of water to a stranger, the sitting down to eat around a cloth, the washing of feet.

"She is one of those people who gets frozen into poise. They become a mirror of themselves, echoes. That is why all she can do is echo me: if I want to live with her, that is what she wants too; if I want to separate, she is willing to accept that too for our sake. She can never do something that is frayed, awry, unexpected. And the pity, bastard, is that she has it in herself—have you looked into those green eyes? I have never seen eyes that color. There is a forest, a lush wilderness trapped in her eyes forever, petrified. She is a prisoner of herself."

"So are you, Ravi," I told him.

"What do you mean?" he retorted, genuinely nonplussed.

"You are trapped in yourself too, or perhaps you could learn to live with her cold poise, for you still do not have any doubts about her love."

He looked at me and blinked. "No," he said, "that is one thing I have no doubts about."

I had read Ravi's story, "A State of Niceness," but I still did not fully understand. I asked him just once. It did not seem kind to ask him again. It was not just the suffering in his eyes that prevented me; it was his need to hide the suffering. But I did ask him once.

"I do not understand," I said to him.

"Understand what?" he replied. "Shakespeare? Proust? Derrida? Ask, ignorant mortal, and thou shalt be answered!"

"You and Lena. If you love her, you know the full-glass version that you gave me, and she loves you, why all this?"

"Because it is the full-glass version," he replied after a moment's hesitation. "You see, my friend, behind any full glass there stretches a vast desert—you have no business quaffing that glass unless you have the courage to go mad in the desert if necessary."

"Beyond me, Ravi," I answered, choosing not to understand him. "But tell me this: whose fault then?"

Ravi laughed.

"You Eng Lit types, you never manage to escape your fucking Milton, do you?"

Then he asked me whether I had seen the film version of *Fiddler on the Roof*. I had not.

"You should," said Ravi. "It is a great musical. You see, it starts with this traditional Jewish family in a small Russian village, just before the Russian revolution. The patriarch—played brilliantly by the Israeli actor Topol—has a number of daughters, all of whom break his ideas of what is right as they grow up and marry. One of them even falls for a communist revolutionary, a man from outside the community. There is a scene where this young communist, recently arrived in the village, has an argument with one of Topol's friends. Topol, who always tries to dialogue even when he disagrees, listens to the young communist's argument and pronounces, a patriarch to his very bones, 'You are right.' Then Topol's friend makes his counter argument and that convinces Topol. 'You are right,' he tells his friend too. Another man standing in the group intervenes. 'He is right, and he is right,' says this third man, 'but they cannot both be right.' Topol thinks about it, looks at the third man and says: 'You are also right.'"

"So?" I asked.

"So, my Miltonic friend," replied Ravi, turning away so as to close the discussion, "you are also right."

I wanted to retort that I could not possibly be right as I had not taken any stand. But it was obvious that Ravi had no wish to talk about the matter anymore.

Just once did I falter in my determination to let Ravi bear his loss—or whatever it was—in his own way. This was on an evening when he had loitered about the flat, cooked something superfluous in the kitchen, gone out, come back and finally ensconced himself on my bed, distracting me from the questions that I was framing for forthcoming exams, and proceeded to turn his mobile over and over again in his hands, as if telling the beads that Karim carried around. I was a bit irritated. I said to him, "Go on, yaar. Why don't you just fucking ring her up?"

"No point," he replied after a pause; a pause so long that I had gone back to setting questions, assuming that Ravi had chosen to ignore my outburst.

"Why? Are you afraid she'll refuse to see you again?"

Ravi smiled a slow, pensive smile. He looked at his mobile.

"It is five forty. Wednesday," he said. "You know, this is about the time she returns from her weekly singing lesson. I don't even need to close my eyes to imagine the world in which she does those things. She walks up the stairs. She stops at her door. She turns the key and goes in, but not before straightening the doormat. She hangs up her coat; she goes into the bathroom to gargle with Listerine. She always gargles with Listerine after singing lessons. I imagine her do these things; I imagine the sounds and smells of her world. No, I don't imagine her; I feel her in my bones, in my flesh. If she were to do anything differently, I would sense it. I would know. So, now, imagine that I call her. Do you know what will happen, bastard?"

"If I were her, Ravi, I would tell you to go to hell."

"If only she would, yaar. If only she would. But no, she won't. She will hear me out; she'll agree to what I suggest. Farewell, last drink together, let's give it another try. She'll agree to any of it in the same even tone. There will be no jarring note from her: not even a go fuck yourself, Ravi!"

What could I have said to that? I returned to framing my questions. Ravi meditated a bit longer on his mobile, turning it around and around. Then he picked up a book of literary criticism and was soon chuckling over it—"This chap makes such a virtue of stating the obvious," he remarked. But he kept the mobile within reach.

THE ISLAMIST AXE PLOT

Then, of course, it happened and I, for one, forgot all about Lena for the next few days. Ravi did not. He could not. But even he soon had other things to worry about. When we had weathered the storm, Ravi did not talk about Lena again to me and probably, given where he is now, to anyone else.

What happened? Well, you can guess. It was front-page news in Denmark. It was reported elsewhere too. But we hardly paid it any attention the morning when it was reported.

Karim Bhai had already left for work. A copy of *Jyllands Posten*—despite all our efforts, Karim Bhai continued to subscribe to this rather provincial paper because he claimed, with some justification, that other national dailies only wrote about Copenhagen—was still lying on the doormat. Karim had obviously left too early to read the paper.

I picked it up and took it to the kitchen. The coffee machine set off its usual infernal racket, which woke up Ravi. He walked in, his sleeping robe loosely tied, rubbing his eyes.

"If this blasted machine did not belong to Karim Bhai," he said, "I would love to use it for target practice."

I still hadn't read the newspaper, which lay on the kitchen table. Ravi sat down and picked it up. Despite his love for cooking, Ravi almost never made breakfast. Actually, though he was not aware of it, he expected coffee to be made and handed to him. I think it was one of those remnants of his past as the only child of rich and famous parents. I wondered what Lena used to make of it. I suspected Danish women would dislike something like that, though I never pointed it out to Ravi: he was a man who strove so much to be what he thought he should be, a man who pushed himself so much, that I thought he was entitled to some habits of relic comfort.

When I handed Ravi his mug of coffee, he was engrossed in the paper. I went to the oven to put in some buns. "Have you read the paper?" he asked.

When I replied in the negative, he laughed and tossed it to me.

"You should read it," he said. "Your brethren have been bothering the blondes again."

On the front page, there was a news item about a Somali man who had assaulted one of the Danish artists who had drawn the controversial Mohammad cartoons a few years back. There was some speculation about the man being part of an Al Qaeda "cell."

This, as we pieced it together, is how it really happened.

It was a few days before Christmas, one of those miserable November days that stretch into February. The little snow on the ground was muddy and sad-looking. A few teenage girls suffered icicle legs in thin stockings for the sake of fashion or boyfriend, but people mostly went about wrapped in jackets and overcoats that had already been beaten out of shape by the winter. The sky had dropped by a few meters, and the clouds reflected the muddy, grimy whiteness of the snow on the ground.

Early morning on a Saturday like this, a Somali man went into a supermarket. It had just opened. The girl at the counter described him as dressed in a weather-beaten overcoat, with layers of woolens underneath. It made him look big and intimidating, though actually he was rather an emaciated, nervous-looking man. He was wearing thick mittens too, and had wrapped his head in a long muffler. He looked distracted, the girl said. He bought a garden axe and a kitchen knife. Later, in another interview, the girl corrected herself and said that he looked "very intense."

From the supermarket, the Somali man walked some blocks to the house of Bent Hansen, retired cartoonist. He stopped once on the way, and sat down on a bench. He was observed by joggers and an old lady retrieving the doings of her poodle: he was trying to sharpen the axe and the knife by rubbing them against each other. It had frightened the old lady away: she had not managed to scoop all her poodle's doings into one of those small plastic bags that she always carried around. It was the first time she had ever broken a law, she told the press at every opportunity.

This sharpening of the weapons of assault was widely discussed in the media, especially on TV. I remember one such discussion. First (male) panelist: It proves that he had intended to murder Herr Hansen. Why else should he sharpen the weapons? Second (male) panelist: It definitely indicates a degree of premeditation. Third (male) panelist: But does one need to sharpen a knife or an axe in order to kill a man? I mean, it is not as if flesh is that resistant or... Hostess (interrupting): Brrr, that's gory... (and turning to the "expert on terrorism"): What would you say, colonel? Expert (male) on terrorism: There is a chance that the accused was specifically influenced by the Taliban brand of Islamism. In all known cases of Islamist assault, axes as well as ceremonial beheadings have been employed by Taliban-influenced militants four times more often than by other jihadist groups...

By and large, media experts agreed that the sharpening of weapons on a street-side bench was an act of premeditation and suggested devious planning. The fact that the Somali left his mittens on the bench also indicated (it was widely noted) that he wanted to retain full use of his hands.

It was not even ten in the morning when the Somali arrived at the house of Mr. Hansen.

Mr. Hansen, a sprightly sixty-nine-year-old man, lived with his wife, who was almost stone deaf and refused to use hearing aids at home. That morning, though, they were babysitting their grand-daughters, two angelic children of seven and nine, as the media photos attest. Or Mr. Hansen was, as Mrs. Hansen had a migraine and was still in bed. The children had insisted on watching an American cartoon and Mr. Hansen had allowed them to do so. The TV was on a bit too loud, but Mr. Hansen did not mind. Tom was chasing Jerry around the house. It kept the girls glued to the screen, which is how Mr. Hansen wanted them to be for another hour or so, after which he planned to take them for a walk in the nearby park. He was in the kitchen fixing a few sandwiches for the park trip when someone rang the bell. Mr. Hansen let it ring a few times as he wrapped the sandwiches in silver foil. But then the person started hammering on the door, and Mr. Hansen could no longer ignore it. He lumbered across the sitting room and past the TV set—where Jerry, having imbibed a potion that he believed gave him superhuman strength, was now chasing Tom around the house—and, absentmindedly carrying a sandwich wrapped in silver foil, went to answer the loud, uncivilized knocking.

When Mr. Hansen opened the door, he realized that the man—an African or Arab, as he told the press in the initial interviews—had not been knocking on the door. He had been trying to break it down with an axe. The axe was still stuck to the door. It had been torn out of the man's hand when Mr. Hansen had opened the door.

The man lunged for the axe handle, shouting something in a language that Mr. Hansen and all his neighbors, some of whom were now peering out of windows, could not understand. But Mr. Hansen knew what it was all about. He heard the word "Mohammad" repeated again and again. He felt the spittle on his face. He had been told what to do in such circumstances. He stayed calm and ran into the bathroom to his left. He closed and locked the door. The bathroom had been reinforced by anti-terror experts: it even had a direct line to the police department. Mr. Hansen called the line as the man—identified as the Somali who had sharpened an axe and a knife on a park bench—started trying to hack down the bathroom door, shouting English words like "revenge" and "honor" along with larger and possibly more complex constructions in some gobbledygook language.

Mr. Hansen had moments of doubt in the reinforced bathroom, though the police took only seven minutes to arrive. He was mostly worried about his grandchildren. He hoped the anti-terror experts were right when they told him that Islamists never attacked family members of their chosen targets. In any case, he knew he was too old to fight a young man armed with a knife and an axe. As he still held one of the sandwiches he had wrapped, he sat down on the toilet seat and unwrapped it. He took a bite from it and waited. The man raged and hammered outside.

Mr. Hansen could hear the TV in the background. A minute before the police arrived, he thought he heard his wife shout to him to get the kids to cut out the racket. When the police arrived, the kids were still watching TV—Tom was back to chasing Jerry around the house—and his wife was sitting up in bed. Despite her deafness, she had heard a bit of the commotion. She later complained to the policemen about how people always made too much noise in the house whenever she had a migraine.

The Somali ran out and threw his axe at the first police car (out of four) that pulled in, sirens blowing. It dented the hood, for which the man will be fined, opined experts on TV, whatever the result of the court case. Then he tried to attack the officers with the kitchen knife. He was easily overpowered and arrested.

"Somali man?" I recall saying to Ravi after I finished reading the article that morning. "Why the hell a Somali? Why not an Afghan, a Paki?"

"Good question, bastard," replied Ravi. "You should hang your head in shame!"

It was hard to take the tragic farce too seriously: media claims of Al Qaeda and conspiracy appeared exaggerated to us. This was needless drama in a land of few incidents, we thought.

Even when Karim Bhai came back and informed us that the Somali in question was Ajsa's Ibrahim, I don't think we suspected what was to come. Karim, I realize in retrospect, was tense and nervous. But then, as we discovered later, he had other reasons too.

Ajsa must have called at least twice that evening. Once, I gathered from Karim's response, someone else called too: I think it was that mystery woman.

The matter got murkier the next day. There were two developments: one of them was a report that had Ali boasting about the Friday Quran sessions that, he claimed, he organized in our flat and where "people of faith discuss what to do in the face of repeated assaults on the Prophet, peace be upon him, by the West." Ali, we were told by the Clauses, who called up to express concern and support, had been on TV last night making similar statements. Evidently, he had been picked up, interrogated, and released by the police, after which—given that Ajsa refused to speak to journalists—he had been interviewed by everyone with a pen or a camera.

The other was an essay by Jens Hauge, a maverick colleague from another faculty, who ranted about "supposed Islamic intellectuals" who abuse Danish hospitality and intrigue against its "democratic principles." It was clear that he had us in mind. I was surprised by how quickly he had managed to write the piece.

Hauge had met Ravi a number of times. Being, in very different ways, among those gaseous satellites of eccentricity that orbit the dense mass of academia, their trajectories had inevitably crossed. But Hauge conveniently forgot that Ravi was, technically speaking, a Hindu. He went on to compare Judaism with Islam and judged the former to be the better religion. I recall that the seriousness of the accusations had not really sunk into us: both of us found the article hilarious. Ravi had remarked, laughing, "This guy has been watching too many WWF matches on TV: Moses vs. Mohammad with Jesus as referee!"

But the smiles were to wear thin on our faces.

It was like the proverbial snowball rolling down a slope. It got bigger and bigger. By the evening we were getting so many phone calls—from media, friends, and strangers—that we stopped answering the phone and even, at times, our mobiles. The public and central registration of information in Denmark had enabled people to get our flat phone number simply on the basis of what Ali had said and what had been reported.

Karim had night duty. He went off looking worried. He had been uncommunicative all day.

I think I started getting seriously worried only when Karim Bhai did not return the next morning. This was not unusual: he might have worked another shift, or he might have been called away by his mystery woman.

Mystery woman? In many ways that was the first time I gave her serious thought. The Danish tabloids were full of suggestions of conspiracy and terror cells. How much did we really know of Karim Bhai? We had moved into his flat on one of Ravi's whims. Who was Karim? Who was the woman? What did he do when he disappeared? What did he do when he was in Cairo?

I was shaken by the fact that all this had not struck us as seriously suspicious in the past.

That night, when Karim had still not returned—he might have called, but we were not picking up the phone—I expressed my doubts to Ravi. He did not dismiss them outright, as I had expected him to. "Let's wait for Karim Bhai to return," he said.

Perhaps that was the best policy. But recall—and if you were in Denmark then, you will be able to recall without any effort—how much publicity Ibrahim's "act of terror" was getting in those days. The Islamist Axe Plot; the Al Qaeda conspiracy. TV, talk shows, tabloids, broadsheets, politicians, police officers, security agents: everyone had an opinion, or spoke in loud ominous silence. The flat was already in the public eye; there were even clusters of people outside our building on occasions. Ali's frequent interviews had ensured that. My colleagues—with some exceptions—pretended they did not know what everyone knew, that I lived in that flat. Our neighbors mostly avoided us.

Did I get paranoid? I don't think so. I do confess that I walked into Karim's room and poked around in it when Ravi was not around. I did not find anything incriminating. But then, I did not expect to. I even looked at the books in his cane bookrack. What was I expecting to find? They were mostly commentaries on the Quran in Urdu and English. The only books of literature I found were a hardback Urdu anthology of selections from Iqbal's poetry, a tattered paperback by Somerset Maugham and Jim Corbett's *The Man-eater of Kumaon*, carefully bound in brown paper.

I am not saying I was uninfluenced by the atmosphere: the "Islamist Axe Plot," as it was being called, was at its height then, with adjectives being flexed and postures struck on all sides. But I still do not think I was paranoid. I had reasons to be suspicious, cause for caution. If you have a Muslim name, you have to be wary in some contexts. Remember the Indian doctor who was arrested and accused of being a terrorist in Australia just because his sim-card ended up in the wrong hands? There are many other stories like that, in Asia, America, Europe. Ravi could afford to ignore them; I could not.

It was I who talked Ravi into going to the police with a full account of our experiences in the flat.

"They will come to speak to us sooner or later," I told him. "It is best that we go to them first."

Ravi did not agree. We had a bit of an argument: this was an issue on which we had never seen eye to eye. Perhaps if Ravi was not still a bit lost as a result of the separation that he had imposed between himself and Lena, he would have refused. Or perhaps, with characteristic generosity, he considered my position as a person with a Muslim name and went along. I know that he let me do most of the talking at the police station.

The main police station in Århus must be one of the calmest, most normal-looking buildings in town. Tucked around the corner from the main bus station, it has no crowds of suspects or uniformed cops hanging around, no patrol cars parked within sight. Actually, when we got off the bus and walked the few steps to the place, I don't think we saw a single person outside the building. Inside, with its counters, brochures and almost total lack of officers in uniform, it looked like any other government office.

Neither Ravi nor I had experienced a police station in India or Pakistan, except as something one drove past. But I am sure both of us associated uniformed people with authority. Even singly, a policeman or an army officer in Pakistan is a bit like a period: sentences stop or start around them. Here, they appeared to be not even a comma; they passed for just another alphabet, indistinguishable from the rest of us.

It was the normality of the place that struck me most. I mentioned this to Ravi while we waited on a bench, after speaking to a woman (was she a cop or a secretary?) at a counter. Ravi muttered some lines—sabse khatarnaak hota hai, murda shanti se bhar jaana, na hona tadap ka, sab sahan kar jaana, ghar se nikalna kaam par, aur kaam se lautkar ghar aana—in a monotone, but he did not say anything else. He was in a dour, uncommunicative mood.

After an initial interrogation by the officers in charge of the station, we were ushered into what looked like a secretary's office, full of nondescript wooden furniture, replete with a tray holding cups, plastic flasks of coffee and tea (labeled) and a bowl of Danish butter cookies. There were even some tabloids and society magazines on a side table. We were then questioned, in greater detail, by two special officers, who did try to get Ravi to speak more at the beginning. But after getting all tied up in his laconic but factual replies—he said the Muslim prayers (Ravi was still "practicing," which he omitted to mention) but no, he was a Hindu, etc.—they offered him a cup of coffee and decided to ignore him.

Of course, the police already knew about Karim's Friday sessions: they had interrogated Ali, Ajsa and probably a few others. But they did not know of his sudden disappearances, his years in Cairo, his need for cash, the mystery caller.

They took my disclosures very seriously.

As I gave an account of our months in the flat, I felt convinced that we were doing the right thing. There was even a moment when I was amazed that we had not seen Karim in his true colors. The occasional secretiveness; the Quran club; the mystery disappearances. The times when he used my laptop: did he only surf for news? A narrow, religious man, intolerant of so many aspects of modernity, could there be any doubt as to his true affinities?

When we returned to the flat, after sharing a couple of silent drinks in a café, Karim had already been arrested. He had returned soon after we went to the police station, and the cops did not have any difficulty picking him up "for interrogation" on the basis of my declarations.

I was told later that they had picked Karim up even as we waited in the police station to sign the printed version of our statements. It must have happened quickly: the necklace of green-black beads and cigarette pouch that Karim always carried around had been abandoned on the kitchen table.

Ravi and I did not want to talk about it. I thought we had done the right thing, but it still felt wrong. Ravi was more affected than me. He murmured about how it all had started resembling the Black Plague years of European history, when the inability to find a reason for sickness and suffering had led to the widespread burning of Jews and strangers. Except that the invisible epidemic this time is capitalism, he grumbled, complicated by the fact that Europeans are accustomed to simply enjoying its advantages. Ravi had never shared my mistrust of Karim's narrow religiosity. Perhaps, also, this was one break too many for him. He had cared deeply for Karim; he had loved Lena from the depths of his ironic soul.

But the flat still glared at us. The note on the fridge, listing in Karim's neat handwriting all the things that had to be bought; the small TV in the kitchen; the coffee machine, which was there only for our use; the half-open door to Karim's room, where his fraying sofa lay empty, sagging, shrouded with his pillows and blankets; the veiled bookrack; the suddenly silent phone in the lobby, the beads on the kitchen table. The flat accused us.

We decided to move out. I don't think we even discussed it. We just started packing. Ravi had already booked his ticket to India: he was leaving in less than a month. He decided to leave his furniture—including the expensive bar—behind. If Karim does not want it, he can throw it out, he said.

We packed the rest of our things. Ravi gave most of his books away to the Clauses and Pernille; he packed them in two boxes and went up to Pernille's flat with them. The next day we rented a storage unit and stored what had to be saved, mostly my furniture, threw out some things and, packing stuff for a week or so, moved into Cabinn.

I had left a curt note for Karim on the kitchen table, telling him that he could adjust this month's rent against our deposit and keep whatever was left over. I had told him to call us on our mobiles if he had questions or differences. He never called.

When Ms. Marx discovered our relapse into Ravi's old gypsy status, she invited us to sleep over at her place the next night.

Ravi got the spare room. I was finally forced to overcome my resistance to sharing her bed when her son was home; the only other option was a sagging sofa in her sitting room.

Yes, you have guessed right: I am still seeing Ms. Marx. I am fond of her son and have even fetched him from school once or twice. That is why I have not named her in this account. I think we are reasonably happy with our half glasses of love. Or I am, in any case. Sometimes I detect a look in her eyes that makes me feel that she is still hoping for something a bit more, and she knows that it cannot be between us. Sometimes I feel her straining against that knowledge.

I don't. I like to hold her in bed; I find the tiny white—they are not blonde—hairs on her arms very sexy; I like the way her thighs, which she considers too thick, swell and fall into trim knees, the way, when she combs her dyed hair, her biceps—which she considers too muscular—jump; I love the dimple she gets when she laughs—which is not often, for she is a serious, busy woman—and I love the slight sag in her belly, left over from childbearing, that she is always trying but unable to get rid of. I love the way she straddles me when we make love, but refuses to let me look at her. I even love her preference for the missionary position.

I am grateful for all this and a hundred other small things. But I am also grateful for the knowledge that she can go on without me and I can continue without her; that, in due course, if required, we might both find our glasses more or less half-full with love for someone else. I will remember her, in that case, as I remember my MFA-girlfriend or my ex-wife, neither more nor less.

That makes me wonder about Ravi, while I sit here typing my version of those days. And about Lena, whom I have glimpsed only occasionally on the campus, smiling, controlled and poised... if Ravi was right about the green depths that hid in her. No, do not misunderstand me: people as accomplished and beautiful as Ravi and Lena always go on too. Of course they will have other relationships. What choice do they have in that matter? I have no doubt of their perseverance. But will a half glass ever suffice for them? A predictable Eng Lit line comes back to me: After such knowledge, what forgiveness?

How Ravi would have scoffed at this quotation. "Fuck, yaar," I hear him laugh. "You Eng Lit types crack me up!"

But let me heed my MFA-girlfriend's advice, this once, and avoid digressions at such a crucial juncture of my account. Let us return to the infamous Islamist Axe Plot.

Like most plots, its tail was twisted, but such twists inevitably become evident only in the end. We slept late the next morning at Ms. Marx's place; by the time we woke up, around nine, she had already dropped her son off at school and picked up fresh bread from a bakery. We had a leisurely breakfast. Ms. Marx and I were teaching later that day; we drove off together. Ravi stayed back. I noticed that he had stopped fiddling with his mobile.

When we returned that evening, I realized that Karim's arrest had distracted Ravi—permanently, I hoped, and said as much to Ms. Marx—from the mantra of his mobile. I don't think he could ever forget Lena, but now he had something else to think about too. He had spent most of the day calling up people who knew us— and Karim. He had even tried to get in touch with Ali, but Ali had not been available. He had called Ajsa, but she was too busy with her own domestic tragedy to have visited Karim in detention. Only Great Claus, it appeared, had visited Karim, who had asked for— and received—his prayer beads in his cell. It appeared that Great Claus and some other people who knew Karim had also spoken to the police.

"It's all a misunderstanding, Great Claus told me," Ravi said to us that evening. "Great Claus says it will become clear soon enough."

I smiled, disbelievingly. I did not want to contradict Ravi, if Great Claus's naïveté made him feel better. Instead, I asked him how Karim had taken to Great Claus's visit; after all, he had avoided the two Clauses ever since they disclosed their homosexuality.

"What do you expect!" Ravi laughed, and I must say it was good to see him laugh again. "Great Claus could not help chuckling over it on the phone. Karim Bhai was touched, he said, but he basically asked Great Claus about his family, his daughters, his job, everything one could possibly think of except Little Claus. As if Great Claus was still living with his family."

Ravi chuckled.

I did not find it funny. I wondered how someone of Ravi's acute intelligence could not draw the obvious inference about Karim's guilt from such, to all eyes, clear proofs of prejudice and narrowness.

POSTSCRIPT TO A PLOT

The very next day, we read in the papers that Karim Bhai had been released. Ms. Marx woke us up with the news before she drove her son to school that morning. She had glanced at the paper, as she always did, while making breakfast for her son. She was as surprised as I was.

I could not possibly drive off without telling you, she said, as we scrambled, bleary-eyed, for the front pages.

Even Ravi could not have been hoping for something so dramatic. Not satisfied with Ms. Marx's daily *Politiken*, he ran off in his pajamas, pulling on a thin jacket and a pair of boots without bothering to put his socks on, and returned in ten minutes—he must have run fast—with all the newspapers and tabloids that he could buy from a neighboring bakery. "Bastard," he cried out, when he saw me again. "What did I say!" He was shivering from the cold, but did not notice it.

Karim had not just been released on bail. It was more dramatic than that. All charges against him had been dropped. There was a photo of him—his back, actually—in one of the tabloids, trying to enter unobtrusively the building in which we had shared a flat with him for a year.

The rest you probably know. Karim Bhai was released after three days in detention; a week later, the police announced that he was not implicated in the "Islamist Axe Plot." The tabloids reported it with barely concealed suspicion. A politician from the Danish People's Party ranted about how weak Danish legislation was, how it allowed terrorists to walk away scot-free. Anti-Muslim online sites such as *Uriahposten* foamed in cyberspace.

But the facts were clear: They had nothing to do with Al Qaeda; they had to do with a Danish woman. Karim had met her in Cairo. She was twenty-three years older than him. They had gotten married.

Seven or eight years ago, when she took early pension, his wife had asked for a divorce. Nothing was wrong between them. I hesitate to say that they were in love, for I wonder whether that much-sullied term holds the same meaning for everyone. But it appears that whatever they had shared in Cairo was still intact.

But Karim's wife had gotten older; perhaps she had another fear at the back of her mind, and wished to release Karim from a burden that she suspected was about to fall on her shoulders. In any case, she felt too old to continue to be in a relationship with a much younger man, a man with other expectations and needs than her. That is what she told him and their mutual friends. She wanted to retire to the countryside, while Karim—she knew—not only needed to be in a city for his work but also, like most colored immigrants in Denmark, felt comfortable only in urban settings.

Karim had differed but he had accepted her decision. They had divorced within a year. He had stayed in touch with her, visiting her regularly as, over the next year or two, it became obvious that she was succumbing to Alzheimer's. When she could not continue to live on her own, Karim Bhai admitted her to the best care he could afford. He went beyond what was freely available under the fraying Danish health-care system, which was being merrily liberalized by successive governments.

Over the years, she had drifted into her own world. Karim Bhai still visited her regularly. In periods when she recovered some lucidity, she would call him, and he would take a day or two off and check into a motel next to her. Those were the phone calls that had increased our suspicion of Karim. Her lucid periods never lasted for more than a day or two. That is when he used to disappear, mysteriously. That is why he would come back looking morose and tired—what Ravi and I, in our final moments of suspicion, read as anger or bitterness. That is why he needed to rent out his flat, work the extra hours.

Of course, the tabloids did not report it in such detail. We heard most of it from the Clauses. As I wrote earlier, we had moved out of the flat—storing most of our stuff in Boxit—the day after we informed on Karim Bhai. We stayed a few days with different friends: three nights at Ms. Marx's, a couple of nights at the Clauses, whose newly conjoined bliss had been dented but not destroyed by the controversy around Karim, a few more nights in other places. Then I found another flat to rent. Ravi had only a few days left in Denmark. He decided to spend them traveling around; when he stayed over in my flat, he slept on a mattress on the floor. We never went back to Karim Bhai's place. It seemed pointless.

But we spoke to common friends and we read the tabloids and papers. The Clauses, in particular, kept Ravi posted.

The papers reported the facts that common friends verified. But the reported facts were stained by incomprehension and suspicion. How could the Danish media really comprehend a man like Karim when we, Ravi and I, had failed to do so? The tabloids sneered subtly at his older-by-more-than-twenty-years wife, insinuating that he must have married her to get into Denmark. But I thought otherwise. I recalled Karim Bhai explaining to Ravi just some months back: "The Prophet, peace be upon him, had only one wife: she was about twenty years older than him. He remained faithful to her and he did not marry again until after she died, peace be upon her."

Why is it that Karim never mentioned to us that he still called on and took care of his ex-wife? It turned out that Great Claus and Pernille had known of her but they were also aware of Karim's strong reluctance to talk about it. So had some other people, but then they did not move in our circles.

Karim had never mentioned staying in touch with his ex-wife—let alone her illness—within our hearing. He had never told anyone who did not already know that he took care of her. He had not even mentioned her existence. Why?

I can give so many answers. Was he embarrassed by her illness, her condition? Or did he feel that silence was owed to the last shreds of dignity to which she still clung in moments of clarity? Did he feel that, being a good Muslim by his own lights, he could not—as my parents would put it—let his left hand know the good that his right hand did? Or was it because—being so narrowly religious—he felt that he was doing something reprehensible and un-Islamic: visiting and spending days alone with a woman who was no longer his wife?

There are other answers too.

But no, they are not answers. They are guesses. Who am I to answer for Karim Bhai? Who are you to demand answers from him?

Lena did not come to see Ravi off at Århus station. I doubt she texted him either.

Yesterday, as I was preparing the manuscript of this book for submission, I received, for the first time since his departure almost a month ago, an email from Ravi. He wrote with no reference to the past. He was in Mumbai. (No, he was in "Bombay," as he actually wrote.) He had refused to move in with his parents; he was working for an NGO and writing as a freelancer. Ravi wrote that he was thinking of going back to journalism in India and uncertain whether he would even return to Denmark to defend his PhD thesis. Despite this old spark of Ravi's fire, it was a subdued email. I heard a voice in it that I could hardly recognize, a resolute but chastened voice, the voice of someone willing to wait for things to happen.

Perhaps that is why I want to add this postscript. I wish to end my account of the infamous Islamic Axe Plot with one of my dreams. My MFA-girlfriend of yore probably had injunctions against ending a factual account with something as unreal as a dream. But a dream it has to be, I feel, for it was a strange dream, which returned me to the beginning of my story. And, more strangely, despite his flippancy and his skepticism, his claim that he never but once dreamed in Denmark, when I think of Ravi, I think of a dreamer. Someone who dreamed so deeply that he could not allow himself to recall his own dreams in the lurid light of ordinary day.

Unlike Ravi, I dream often and incoherently. I sometimes remember the shards and pieces of my dreams beyond those seconds of fleeting lucidity that divide sleep from wakefulness but dissolve in the glare of day. This dream too slipped from my memory, and returned only yesterday—triggered perhaps by Ravi's email or by a glimpse of Karim. I need to talk about both.

I had the dream the night Ravi left; I'd accompanied him to Copenhagen. We had friends there, and it seemed a good idea to hit the town in order to see him off. As Ravi's flight to Amsterdam left at six in the morning, we had less than three hours of sleep after our evening out with friends. Around four we took a taxi to the airport; we were too bleary-eyed to take the tube or the bus, as we had originally intended. We left as quietly as we could, for we did not want to wake up the hung-over friends at whose place we had slept. We did not say much in the taxi either, or at the airport. After checking in, Ravi gripped me by the elbow and took the escalator into the security clearance sections of Kastrup.

I hung around, walking about the orderly, compact airport, and then buying myself an elaborate and slow breakfast. Around nine, I caught a train back to Copenhagen's central station and from there, a little later, to Århus. It was a bit after three when I reached Århus. It was a Sunday; the town was largely deserted. A bit of snow had fallen. The parked cars and cycles looked like they had been dusted with talcum powder. I walked down the pedestrian street, stopping to have a shawarma sandwich and a coke at a small Turkish eatery; a bitter wind was blowing from the sea, chilly with the ice of the North. I felt the kind of exhaustion, exacerbated by lack of rest and drinking the night before, which demands but does not permit sleep.

The early winter night had fallen, darkening the streets, when I finally reached the small, freshly painted two-room university apartment I had rented at the campus after moving out of Karim's flat. I tried to read a book but could not concentrate. I opened a bottle of red wine but had little desire to drink. Around eight, without warning, sleep descended on me in a swarm of tiredness, with the sensation of a flock of crow-like birds, of a dark cloud falling from the sky, and I just managed to reach the bed before falling asleep. I do not recall the night. And when I woke up, a bit too early next morning, the dream too had misted in my memory. It came back only yesterday, with Ravi's email and a disturbing glimpse of Karim: two living ghosts who continue to haunt me, it seems. I think I saw Karim Bhai's taxi yesterday. I was returning from Ms. Marx's place; her son is with her this week and I always feel odd sleeping over when he is home, though she has no objection to it. It was not too late, perhaps a bit after ten at night. The roads were crowded with young people—improbably dressed, especially the women in their stockings and tights, despite the cold—and I wanted to escape the forced clockwork bonhomie. Ravi and his desperation to live without being lost in habit was on my mind. I walked briskly to a taxi stand and spotted what I thought was Karim's cab parked there. I dodged into another street. Urbanity provides us with so many ways to avoid people. Isn't that what distinguishes it from traditional rural life, where the onus, perhaps because it was difficult and rare, was more on greeting people?

I walked half a kilometer to another stand, wondering why I had avoided Karim. Was I ashamed of facing him again? Perhaps. But I think it was more than that. I was ashamed of facing him and not being able to apologize fully. I felt we had done him an injury by preferring our suspicions—and I was more responsible for this than Ravi—to the daily evidence that he had provided of courtesy and decency within the limits of his humanity. But it wasn't even that: not apology, which was neither demanded nor required, but honest conversation was impossible now.

How could I talk to him—I more than Ravi—again? It is, after all, Karim's kind of religion that is used by fundamentalists of a different sort to condone the murder of innocent passers-by, the incitement of young men and women to commit acts whose brutal consequences they are hardly aware of at times. It is his kind of literal reading of the Quran that is used by Islamists to justify beheadings or the veiling of women, and, strangely, by those who hate Islam to dismiss an entire and complex tradition. It is the same Towhid—so precious to Karim—that jihadists use to espouse an intolerance so extreme, an order so narrow that only someone like

Ravi, with his insistence on the anti-universalism of fascism, could distinguish it from fascism. How could I have spoken with a clean heart to Karim Bhai? Too much stood between him and me, and there was no Ravi—with his mocking belief in all that is best in us—to bridge the chasm now.

Guilt, you say? No, guilt is too glib a word, too simple—the sort of answer demanded of, and sometimes given by, novelists. Ravi might have felt some guilt for giving in to what, I suspect, he finally considered my fears for my own safety rather than his own opinion of Karim Bhai. But guilt is not what I felt, or not mainly. After all, I had not turned Karim over for interrogation by the Pakistani or Indian police, or sent him to Abu Ghraib! All I had condemned him to was relentless questioning, over cups of coffee perhaps, by orderly Danish investigators, no matter how prejudiced—questioning that, I am sure, would have come his way in any case, given his name and location. Think of the "Norway attacks" last year and the confidence of Danish journalists in attributing them to Islamists: what kind of people do you think would have been picked up for questioning if it had not been discovered that the perpetrator was a light-eyed, light-skinned Norwegian? No, guilt is not the word.

What I felt was the impossibility of conversation, as if I would have to shout across a Niagara of noise to Karim Bhai and what would come across, if anything, would not be the words I meant or the words he uttered but a sort of crude pantomime. It was not that we did not wish to talk. But the Niagara of suspicion and prejudice and brashness cascading around us made honest conversation impossible between the two of us.

No wonder I took advantage of the many avenues of urbanity to shirk facing Karim. And perhaps it was this conscious decision to avoid Karim which returned from my unconscious that dream I had the night Ravi left for India.

I was in Mumbai airport in my dream. I had just landed there with Ravi. Mumbai airport was a mishmash of every airport in the world that I had ever traversed: Karachi, Islamabad, Lahore, Copenhagen, Stansted, Heathrow, Paris, Munich, Moscow, Billund and half a dozen others. This was inevitable. I had never been to Mumbai: my only trip to India had been via Delhi. But despite the mishmash and its ever-changing chameleon features, I knew this airport to be Mumbai.

Ravi had a smart little backpack: he always traveled light. I was bowed down with bulky hand baggage and dragging a huge suitcase whose wheels squeaked at regular intervals. Consequently, Ravi often left me behind and then had to wait for me to catch up.

We were heading out of the arrivals section of the airport. A small boy went past us, dragging a striped towel, and—with the sudden critical lucidity of dreams—I recognized the boy as walking out of my favorite comic strip, *Peanuts*, though he also seemed familiar in some other vague manner. He made me notice something in my dream. It appeared that everyone else, like the boy, was heading the other way; and when Ravi stopped, I asked him if we were going in the right direction. He nodded and we kept walking, the suitcase emitting piercing squeaks which almost woke me up.

Ravi was right. We came within sight of the exit. There were the usual armed policemen next to it. There was the usual crowd outside, and noise spilling like sunshine. People were jostling each other, eager for passengers to come out; there were taxi drivers, relatives with children, acolytes carrying garlands waiting for some godman, politician, cricketer or film star, and dozens of people holding name placards, some held high on sticks. It could have been Delhi or Karachi, but I knew it was Mumbai.

Ravi had left me behind again. I stopped. He turned around and peered at me quizzically, an eyebrow raised ironically, as he sometimes did.

Look, I said to him and pointed to the exit, which had suddenly come closer. Outside, the taxi drivers, relatives, acolytes, tourist guides, placard-bearers had metamorphosed into a mob.

They were still staying in place, behind the metal barricades. But the placards had changed into weapons: trishuls, spears, lathis, crescent-shaped swords. It was the same noise, though, spilling around us like the brilliant sunshine outside. All these people were still waiting to receive us, it appeared. Some were even smiling. But now, in place of placards, they were waving weapons and flags: green flags, saffron flags, white flags.

Ravi looked at the mob and turned back to me. He shrugged his shoulders and made a gesture for me to follow him. But I stood where I was. He looked again at me, the same quizzical look, eyebrow raised. I shook my head.

Ravi laughed. He had a clear, hearty laugh. The airport rang with it in my dream. Then, still laughing, he walked into the crowd of weapons raised to greet him, the noise and sunshine that swallowed him in a split second.

I looked around and realized that I was not in Mumbai airport after all. I was in a car, a Hyundai i10 parked on Kastelsvej, holding a small plastic container. On the container was a label with a name written on it which I could not read: the name never ended no matter how much I revolved the container. I knew I did not have the time to keep revolving the container. I had to keep the engine running, waiting for my chance. I knew I had to be quick. Dawn was about to break. A sliver of sunshine would pierce the overcast sky and fall on the wet, grey earth. I had to be fast. I had to fill my plastic container with the meager sunshine that would penetrate the clouds, fall fleetingly on the ground. I doubted it would be sufficient. I feared it would never be sufficient.

I remember thinking in my dream, even as I woke up feeling thirsty, that it is not just manufacturers of plastic containers who overestimate the capacity of man.

ACKNOWLEDGMENTS

Thanks are due to Isabelle Petiot, for her generous understanding and feedback; to Sébastien Doubinsky, Indra Sinha, Matt Bialer, Mita Kapur, Caspian Dennis, V.K. Karthika, Ellen Dengel-Janic, Maria Beville, Aamer Hussein, Sharmilla Beezmohun, Renuka Chatterjee, Shashi Tharoor, Mohsin Hamid, Nicole Angeloro, Shantanu Ray Chaudhuri, Saugata Mukherjee, Charlotte Day, Etgar Keret, Jim Hicks, Michel Moushabeck, Hilary Plum, Zac O'Yeah and Ole Birk Laursen for feedback and faith; to Jamal Bhai, Dominic, Matthias, Christopher, Joe and Simon for coffee and conversation; to Hana Hasanbegovic, Jane L. Didriksen and Afsir Mama for a word each in three different languages; and to a host of "Eng Lit" writers, mostly dead, for necessary echoes, sometimes even duly acknowledged.